THE SMURFS TALES

Peyo

PAPERCUTZ
NEW YORK

THE SMURFS TALES #4

"Smurf and Turf"
BY PEYO
WITH THE COLLABORATION OF ALAIN JOST AND THIERRY CULLIFORD FOR THE SCRIPT, PASCAL GARRAY FOR THE ARTWORK, NINE CULLIFORD FOR THE COLORS

"The Goblin of Rocky Wood"
BY PEYO

"Spells at the Castle"
BY PEYO

"Enguerran the Valiant"
BY PEYO

"The Super Smurf"
BY PEYO

"The Smurf Gags"
BY PEYO

Joe Johnson, *SMURFLATIONS*
Bryan Senka, *LETTERING SMURF*
Léa Zimmerman, *SMURFIC PRODUCTION*
Matt. Murray, *SMURF CONSULTANT*
Jeff Whitman, *MANAGING SMURF*
Jim Salicrup, *SMURF-IN-CHIEF*

HC ISBN 978-1-5458-0871-9
PB ISBN 978-1-5458-0872-6

PRINTED IN MALAYSIA
APRIL 2022

Papercutz books may be purchased for business or promotional use. For information on bulk purchases please contact Macmillan Corporate and Premium Sales Department at (800) 221-7945 x5442.

DISTRIBUTED BY MACMILLAN
FIRST PAPERCUTZ PRINTING

SMURF
AND TURF

The Smurfs lead a very peaceful life. They're not, however, immune to overwork. Granted, that's rather hard to believe...
Will you help me move my armoire?
Yes, but it'll be time to eat soon. Let's smurf that after our nap.
Tailor Smurf, I'll be needing new pants.
Will next month work?
?

Now, let's observe Handy Smurf, who's working on a new invention.
That should smurf this time...
CLAP

PSHHHHT
First, I need pressure...
Hup!

Now I smurf the cherries into the machine...

There! The stems are coming out already.

Now the pits!
PLING
PLING

Next the cherries...
?!
SPLET
SPLET
SPLET
PLING
1

Dangsmurfit! They're completely smurfed. I just don't get it.
What's that contraption?

A cherry desmurfer!
A WHAT?!

A machine to smurf cherry pits! I'm speaking smurf, you know!
Whoa! Calm down!

You need to fix the door to the bread oven! It has smurfed off its hinges!

It can't wait?
No, it can't wait! I have to smurf my bread!

This is annoying. I can never smurf in peace.

Handy Smurf, have you smurfed my wheelbarrow?
No, not yet.

And my lawnsmurfer?
I'll smurf you when it's ready.

Can you smurf a look at my cuckoo clock? It's not going cuckoo, it say
NO TIME!

I'll be the one getting unhinged one of these days!
2

Hey, can you fix my smurf-masher?

1in/in²
PLOP

Smurfreka! I think I've got it!

I have to smurf the bobbin of the centrismurf regulator...

CHOOOF
CHOOOF
There are the stems... the pits...
PLING
PLING

Well, where are the cherries?

Are they coming out?!
BAM
BAM

SPLAT

Smurfblasted machine! I'm going to--
I came to get my ax.

NOW'S NOT THE TIME!
But I need it for smurfing in the forest.

For smurf's sake! You could smurf a new handle on it yourself!
BING
BING
BING

HERE'S YOUR AX!
3

And my wheelbarrow?
And my smurf-masher?
And my lawnsmurfer?
And my waffle-smurf?
And my smurf mill?
And my clothes smurf?
?
And my smurf desmurfer?

RHAAAAA

What a horrible sound! It smurfs like a dying animal!

Keep a safe distance! Handy Smurf has smurfed a gasket.

I'VE SMURFED IT UP TO HERE! FIX THEM YOURSELVES!

And that r you, you
BING
BING

HFFF! PFFF! HFFF!
Handy Smurf, I think we need to talk...

I don't know what got into me. There's that machine that refuses to smurf... And the others smurfing after me all day long...

I suddenly smurfed red... I lost my smurf.

You just smurfed an emotional outburst, that's all. You're way too tense.

Maybe you could smurf a cure for me... You know all the plants...
No, that won't solve anything.

What you need is rest. No more inventing, no more odd jobs... No smurfing anything at all.

Not smurfing anything... That'll be hard, Papa Smurf.
Certainly not. I'll tell everyone to smurf you a break.

And stop smurfing yourself sick. A machine for desmurfing cherries isn't a critical need.
Oh? You don't think so?

So, has he calmed down?
What smurfed into him?
He's not dangerous, at least?

Listen, Handy Smurf is overworked. He must smurf total rest. So you won't ask for anything else, got it?
Yes, Papa Smurf.
5

I sure slept late this morning.

What a joy it is not hurrying while smurfing my breakfast.

Now I'm going to smurf a little walk along the river.

Still, it's too bad! Such a lovely machine...

Meh! Let's forget about it. The sun's shining, the birds are smurfing...

Hey! Your shutter has smurfed off!
Oh, it's no big deal...

I'll smurf it back on myself. It's easy, I know what I'm doing.
Oh? Okay!
TCHIRP
TCHIRP

?
!
TCHIRP
TCHIRP
TCHIRP

The wheel is squeaking. We should smurf some grease here on the hub...
Oh, yes. No worries, I'll take care of it.

Okay, see you later!
TCHIRPTCHIRPTCHIRP
TCHIRPTCHIRP
6

Hello! What are you smurfing?
Oh, nothing. I'm fixing a little gap in the wall.

Your mixture is too watery. You need to smurf more cement in it.
Oh? Okay.

Come on, that's not how you smurf it. You're smurfing your time.

Smurf me that. I'm going to show you how.

Oh? Handy Smurf is feeling better.
Yes! He's smurfed back to work!

Hey, can you fix my easel?
And my smurfophone?

No, no! Go away! I said to smurf him a break!

This won't smurf like this! You must smurf far away from here, have a change of scene!

Tell me, don't you know some quiet place where you'd like to rest?
Uh...

I like the big lake in the mountains a lot. I could smurf there for a few days...
Great idea!
7

There! I think I have everything.

Hey, don't you want me to come with you? I'll help you carry all that.
No thanks, Hefty Smurf. That's nice of you, but I'll be fine.

Do you think he can smurf that trip on his own?
Oh, yes, it'll smurf him good.

Papa Smurf is right! I have to smurf a little distance.

From up here, everything seems less important.

I love walking. I could smurf like this all day long.

My backpack is heavy. I smurfed too much stuff.

Pfff! I should have smurfed a little exercise before going.

Let's go... make an effort... I have to... smurf there... before... nightfall.
8

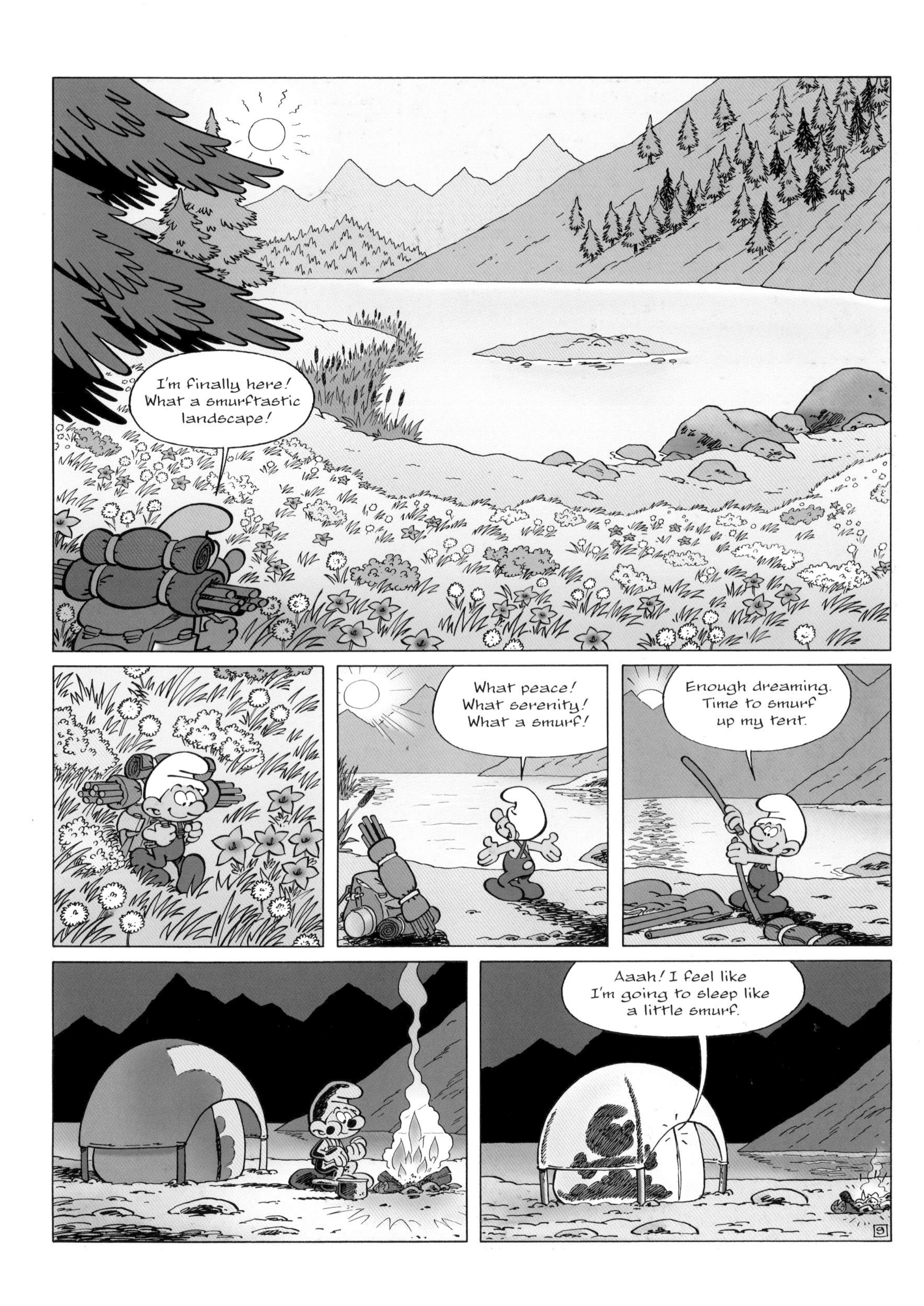
I'm finally here! What a smurftastic landscape!
What peace! What serenity! What a smurf!
Enough dreaming. Time to smurf up my tent.
Aaah! I feel like I'm going to sleep like a little smurf.
9

I feel smurfily great! Any time I get tired, I'll come smurf a few days here.

That smurfs me an idea! I have to smurf a little sketch.

My pencil! Darn! Where did I smurf my pencil?! I really was distracted!

This stick will do the job.

There, something like that... I'll smurf to work tomorrow morning.

A few days later...

I smurfed a pie for Handy Smurf. He's coming back today, isn't he?
Oh, he won't be much longer.

TRA LA LALA LA LAAA

There he is now! And he looks like he's in a good mood.
Hello, everybody! How's it smurfing around here?

Hello, Handy Smurf. Did everything smurf well?
Yes, Papa Smurf. That was an excellent idea of yours.
10

Thanks for the pie, Smurfette. I'll eat a piece and smurf back to work.

Uh... Are you sure you're okay? You just smurfed a long walk...
I'm in excellent shape, Papa Smurf.

That stay at the lake smurfed me a world of good! In fact, I'm planning on going back regularly.
Oh?

Oh, yes, your easel... No worries. Come smurf it in a bit.
What a change. It's incredible.

Geez... Handy Smurf is weird!
Yes, he seems TOO happy!

I'll bet my bottom smurf he's hiding something from us!
When I go back to get my easel, I'll try to smurf the truth out of him.

Here, I smurfed a new one that's collapsible. The other one is too smurfed.
Oh... Thanks.

Hey, you're as happy as a smurf... There must be a reason.
You know you can smurf us anything...
Hmm!

Well... I smurfed myself a little house beside the lake.

Another house? Far from the village?!
Nobody has ever smurfed that!

Hey, we'd really like to see your house.
Could we smurf there with you?
Okay, but let's smurf this between us. I don't want everyone talking about it!
11

He smurfed himself a house beside the lake?
And he's going back there in a few days.
What?! That's not serious.
Painter Smurf and Poet Smurf are going to smurf there with him.
?
I have to smurf Smurfette about this.

So, are you ready?
Yes, let's go!
We're impatiently smurfing!

See you soon! We're going to smurf up there for three days!

Smurfing all that way to go to a lake where there's nothing to smurf...
What an idea!
Me, I don't like lakes.
We can rest very well right here. In fact, I'm going to smurf a little nap... ->Yawwwn!<-

What's more, he didn't invite us.
That's true. That's not very smurf of him.

Meanwhile, at the edge of the forest...
Azrael, our revenge is at hand!
12

I just found an impressive spell! The days of those cursed Smurfs are numbered!
?

Here's my refuge...
I smurfed it with material from here: earth, straw, and reeds.

We can smurf food outside here, sheltered from the sun and rain...

Oh! There's even--
Yes! All the conveniences.

Your house is as smurf as can be!
Isn't it? But with three of us, we'll have to smurf a little.

It doesn't matter. The location is smurfily beautiful!

In fact, I'm going to set up my easel and smurf a drawing.
I feel my inspiration starting to smurf, too.

Come look!
I smurfed a surprise for you...
13

There! A little imagination and the tour is smurfed.

Smurf me a hand to get it in the water.

This is so nice! I wish it smurfed like this always...
O smurf! Arrest your flight!

You were right, Handy Smurf! This place is magical!

Handy Smurf, we have one question to smurf you...

We wouldn't want to bother you, but...
Would you mind if we smurfed ourselves a little house, too?

You know... There's no lack for smurf beside the lake.

Okay! I'll smurf you how--
HURRAY!
14

After all, I'm the one who smurfed up with that idea of going to the mountain...

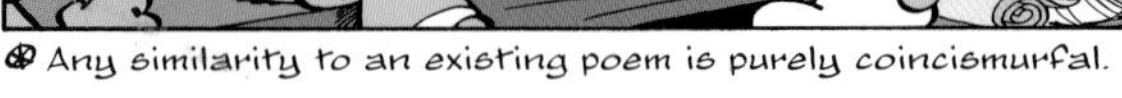
⊛ Any similarity to an existing poem is purely coincismurfal.

WE WANT TO SMURF TO THE LAKE, TOO!

Wait, that's not so smurfy! You understand... Uh...

Come, we have to smurf among ourselves.

It's not possible. We smurfed three little houses... We can't invite all of them.
Then two or three at a time.
Yes, but in what order?

We could smurf straws... Or smurf a lottery.
Or invite those who are the smurfiest with us.

I'll start by inviting Smurfette.
And why you? My house is smurfer than yours is.

Stop squabbling! We have to smurf them a final answer otherwise we'll never smurf the end of it!

It's simple: everybody can't smurf to the lake, period!

You should be ashamed!
That lake isn't yours!
You're selfish!
And I'll tell Papa Smurf!
17

Oh! Handy Smurf!
Where are you smurfing like that?

They're right. If they want to smurf up there, it's their right.

It's up to me smurf a solution. But that'll require a lot of thought...

Late into the night...
Z
Z

And, early in the morning...
You understand, I'd like to smurf each one the chance to enjoy that magnificent place.
Uh... That's very smurf of you.

To accomplish my plan, I'd just need a team of volunteers to smurf me a hand...
?

So basically, here's the idea!
Oh, yeah... Wow!

Thanks for smurfing me your approval, Papa Smurf. I knew I could smurf on you.
?

I didn't have the heart to tell him no... But I wonder where all this will smurf us.
18

There we go! All the ingredients are ground and crushed... My magic powder is ready!

If the formula works, it will turn you into a true bloodhound! An extraordinary hunting dog!
!

Come out from there, now! You won't really be changed into a dog! And besides, the effect only lasts a few hours...
HISSS!

I said: come out from there! You must help me hunt the Smurfs!
MEOOOW!
KRR

There, there... Already done!
PFFF
PFFF

ATCHOO!

Meow... Mwoof!
Ah ha! It's working!

WOOF
WOOF
WOOF

Now we just have to run around the forest wherever the sarsaparilla grows... With your nose, it won't take us long to flush out our prey!

Let's go, search, you good do--uh... you good cat! Don't forget that your sense of smell won't last forever!
SNIF
SNIF

Have you smelled something?! There's smurf in the air! HA! HA! HA! HAAA!
SNIF
SNIF
SNIF
19

Good... Good... The trail's getting clear!
SNIF SNIF

Are they there? Behind the bush? We musn't alert them!

!

A mole! Do you think I'm looking for a fur collar?! You're as useless a dog as you are a cat!

Meanwhile, at the lake...

Goodness me all this work is exsmurfing.

Hang in there! As volunteers, you'll be the first ones to smurf vacation here.
What is vacation?

It's what you deserve when you've smurfed a good job.
Oh?

So, to have vacation, you must work first?
There's always a catch with these modern things!
20

Papa Smurf, I want to smurf to the lake with the first group!
Me too, Papa Smurf!
Me too!

Wait, we must get organized so the village will continue to smurf normally!

Those who most need rest will smurf first!
Me, Papa Smurf!
And why you?

Why?! For smurf's sake! You go try to see how to smurf vegetables by the sweat of your brow!

What about me, then? You think hauling bags of seeds and flour is Baby Smurf work?
And smurfing bread is as easy as pie?

It's already getting complicated. I have to smurf my calm...
Papa Smurf!

It's an invitation to the lake. We're smurfing on you for the inauguration.
Already? Hmm...

I propose that Smurfette replaces me for the ceremony. I'll smurf up there later...
Oh... Thanks, Papa Smurf!

And soon...
Smurfette, here are the scissors.
Hee! Hee! Hee!

The honor of smurfing the ribbon is all yours.
21

HURRAY FOR THE SMURF AND TURF SPA!
CLAP CLAP
CLAP CLAP CLAP
CLAP CLAP
CLAP CLAP
CLAP
SNIP

Great job, Handy Smurf!
You smurfed a wonderful project!
SMACK
Thanks, thanks...

You're invited to smurf a raspberry juice to celebrate the event. And I'll smurf new arrivals the number of their huts.

You'll have #4! And you, #5...
Oh, we're neighbors!

He'd better not smurf any noise at night... We're here to rest.
I hope I won't hear him snoring at night.
You'll smurf up to #12, on the hill.
What? I'm not beside the water?!
22

Ah! You've got to admit, we're smurfily well off here.
Yes! And it's a good place for Smurf-watching!

It's hot. I sure could smurf another raspberry juice...
Me too!

Are you going to smurf us one?
Why me? It was your idea.

I'm looking for volunteers. We have to go smurf wood for cooking.
Oh, no! Not me!
Me neither!

Then you'll have to help prepare the meal. Or to smurf the dishes. The work won't get smurfed all on its own.

If we have to smurf all those chores, it's not a vacation anymore.
That's right. We're here to rest.

This won't smurf like this. We need another system...

HELLO, HELLO! ANNOUNCING TO ALL SMURFS!
?

Please smurf to the music gazebo for the drawing! I repeat...

Cool! I love lotteries!
Me too, but I never smurf anything...
23

I smurfed all the hut numbers in this basket. Smurfette's innocent hand is going to smurf out six at random...
Hee! Hee! Hee!
What's the big prize?
Hey, what do we smurf?

Might as well tell you right away... We're smurfing the list of those who are going to work till tomorrow.
What?! You've got to be smurfing us!
I'm out of here!

Think about it. You just have to smurf a day of service. Afterwards, we'll change teams, and you can really enjoy your vacation.

Hmm. Maybe he's not wrong.
If there's no way to smurf otherwise...
Okay, let's smurf the drawing.

Nine, six... seven...
Well, smurf, I won.
Me ...me too! That's never happened before.
Consmurf-ulations!

And so...
Vanity Smurf, a berry juice, please!
SNAP

Hmm! This juice isn't very cold...
What a smurfer he is! He's never happy!

Vanity Smurf, I'd like one last berry juice.

Sorry, my shift is over.

And I advise you to get to bed! Tomorrow, you'll be the one smurfing breakfasts.
24

Early the next morning...
Hmm... This herbal tea isn't very hot.
What a smurfer he is!

Enough smurfing in bed! I must enjoy the day.

First, a dip in the lake!

And hup!

Look out where you're smurfing! Are you trying to sink my boat?

Those gondoliers are smurfing! I'll go lie beside the pool.

What? All the places are already smurfed?!

Too bad! I'll smurf the morning on the beach.

There's room here at least.

I wonder why they're all smurfing in the same spot.
25

Do you want my umbrella, Smurfette?
Your swimsuit is absolutely smurf!
Aren't you thirsty?
A little suntan lotion?

Excuse me, I'll be right back!

They're nice, but a little smurfsistant!

Oh, hello, Smurf!
?

Hey, are you smurfing anything special this morning?
Uh... No, Smurfette, nothing at all!

Well, I feel like going to the far end of the lake, it's calmer there. I can smurfbathe in peace.
Oh, yes! That's a smurftastic idea!

Isn't it? Then you won't mind taking care of Baby Smurf till I get back?
Aroo!
!

Gaa! Gaaa!
You said it!
26

What a pleasure to be on vacation. No more Smurfs to serve, no platter, no apron...

Today, I can put my smurfs up and enjoy the sunshine at my leisure.

At my leisure... Hey, that smurfs me an idea!

Whoaaaa! Take a smurf at that!
TAP TAP

What are those pants?
The water's gone to his brain!
Ha! Ha! Haaa!

Good ol' Vanity Smurf! As smurf as ever!

Oh, Vanity Smurf! What a smurfastic outfit!

It smurfs you beautifully! How do you smurf up with such awesome ideas?

Later...
PFFFFRT!
What?! Have you seen yours? Take a smurf at yourself in the mirror!
27

Hey! The information booth is open.

Say, do you know what they're smurfing tonight at the gazebo?
No! What?

What do you mean what? I'm smurfing you that question.
I don't know anything about it.

Oh, come on! They said they'd smurf a show at the gazebo every night.
Oh? That's news to me...

Well, geez, what are you smurfing at this information booth?
Handy Smurf is the one who told me to smurf here all day long... And you're wearing me out with your questions!
Hey there! Quiet down! We'd like to smurf in peace!

You have to be smurf to get mad like that.
For real. We're on vacation for once...
POC

The lake, the sunshine, no bread to smurf... I'm savoring every minute.

I'll tell you what makes me the happiest...

...it's that down there in the village, they must smurf along without us.
I bet they have a mess on their hands!
Yes... Ha! Ha! There's got to be trouble!
28

In the village, in fact...
Papa Smurf, I have to smurf you something!

Look at this bread! Do you think it's smurfable?
Uh, it looks a little oversmurfed.

It's like that every time ever since Potter Smurf smurfed Baker Smurf's place.

Usually I smurf jugs and plates! I know diddly-smurf about cooking bread.

Now, now, don't get angry! Try to smurf another batch!
I'd be glad to, but we're out of flour!

Out of flour... Oh, my! There's no sub for Miller Smurf!
No, but you're smurfing me from me!

Look here, are you smurfing me? You didn't soak them... And that's zucchini, not cucumbers!
I'm smurfing what I can! Gardening's not my smurf!

A little patience! Everything will smurf back in order once Farmer Smurf comes back...

Maybe! But I'm warning you, once he's back, I'm the one who'll be going! I'm a smurf-wreck!

For smurf's sake! Who could sub for Chef Smurf?!
29

Papa Smurf, I think that it's my turn go to the Smurf and Turf Spa!
What? So, you're tired, too?

No, but someone serious-minded must go see what's smurfing on up there... I'll smurf you information.

Sure, go ahead! I know you're a good informer.

Z

And you? You don't feel like going on v ation, by any c ce?

Yes, Papa Smurf, I dream of it. But smurfing all the way there is exhausting. So, I'm hesitant...

There, it's ready!

The ingredients are hard to find, but this time I was able to prepare a good dose. The hunt for the Smurfs can resume!
PFFF...

What?! Trying to sneak out?
SLAM

Azrael, your lack of cooperation really hurts me!

TCHOOF TCHOOF
Atchoo!
30

And this time, make an effort!
Woof.

Nothing yet? Think about the smell of Smurfs... You've had some right under your nose before!

Ah?! Have you found a trail?
SNIF
SNIF
SNIF SNIF

Sarsaparilla! We're close this time!

There! I see some leaves moving...

AND BAM! A good haul!
FROOOSH

A... a weasel!?
?

What a stink! That little monster sure got us!

Azrael! Come take a bath or I'll send you to live with the weasel!
WOOF! MEOW!
31

At the Smurf and Turf Spa, the nights are lively...

...and the mornings are calm...

Some are taking it slow...

...while waiting for the moment of suspense...

Others are taking initiative...

Vanity Smurf is as creative as ever...

Brainy Smurf tries to raise the cultural level...

Strange practices appear...

Here's a smurftastic place for a picnic with Smurfette.

Well, darn! My oar is stuck in the mud.

SPLOTCH

Ha! Ha! What a smurf!
He fell out of his boat!
NOT AT ALL! Mudbaths are very smurfy for your skin, everysmurf knows that!

Yuck! It's disgusting!
Yes, but very smurfy for your skin!
SPLITCH SPLATCH
SPLOTCH

Basically, they're all happy on their vacation. Although...
MOVE!
I HAVE RIGHT OF WAY!
And then the Smurf answered: "Yes, but I've lost weight!"
HAHAHA
WAAAAH
PLAF
PLOF
PLITCH PLATCH
OH SMURFAY MIIIO...
What's he smurfing?!
One evening, do you recall, we were smurfing in silence...
That's ancient history, buddy!

That's true, Painter Smurf... It's not like it was before. All this hustle and bustle has smurfed my inspiration.

I'm not painting anything anymore either! What's more, what with all this construction, the loveliest landscapes are smurfed!

To be honest, I feel like smurfing back to the calm of our village...
You too? How about we leave tomorrow?

At the village...
When can we go, Papa Smurf?
That's right. Summer won't smurf forever!

We must wait for the first group to come back... But I don't have any news.
I'm tired of waiting!

I'm sorry, but if they don't come back, I'm smurfing everything and leaving!

I'm tired, too! Everything is smurfing badly in the village! So, here's what I've decided...

Vacation for all! We'll smurf our bags and all go!
HURRAY!
Hurray for Papa Smurf!

At last, our dear old village!

But... What are they smurfing?

What, you're all smurfing the village?
And we're coming home!

It's just as well. You could stay here and smurf an eye out.
Uh... If you like, Papa Smurf.

Okay then! If anything smurfs, let me know at the Smurf and Turf Spa!
34

We'll have plenty of peace and calm.
What a relief! I wouldn't smurf a little nap.

I heard Handy Smurf made himself a smurfily comfortable bed...
Try it out! We're the guards, we can smurf where we like!

En route...
We're not moving! What's smurfing?
Clumsy Smurf lost his stuff on the way.
And Grouchy Smurf twisted his ankle. They have to smurf him a bandage.
Over his mouth?
We all shouldn't have left at the same time.
That's right! Spreading out the departures would have been more... let's say, smarter.
Me, I don't like bandages!

And at the Smurf and Turf Spa...
They've all smurfed from the village? And where are they?
On the way! You have time to get organized!

But you're already here, Papa Smurf?!
I came by stork! You know, smurfing a long walk, at my age...

The stork is a good idea! It's fast and less tiring... We could travel farther without smurfing so much time...
This little house is very pretty.

Meanwhile, what's to be done to house all the Smurfs at the same time?

I'll have to smurf urgent measures!
35

That night...
It's so hot! And these mosquitoes are driving me smurf!

Stop smurfing like that. You're making the whole bed shake!
Smurf me alone, you!

Hey, can you two smurf less loudly? I'd like to sleep!
Oh, all right!

GRATT GRATT
What a night! I must smurf my head in the pool to wake up!

But... That's not a pool! It's Smurf soup!

-PFFF!- I need air. I'm going to smurf a boat ride on the lake.

A boat? But it's not that simple... You have to smurf a reservation.

Let's see... I can smurf you one in the evening the day after tomorrow!
?
FLAP

If this is what vacation is like, it's not what I'd smurfed! Let's see what we're smurfing at noon...
MENU
Today

Nettle soup, mashed turnips, dandesmurf salad... Oh, come on! What's with this menu?!
Don't you get it? With all these meals to smurf, we're running short on food!
And don't complain... You're not the one who had to smurf the nettle soup!
36

Snirf!

I know, poor Azrael... You caught a nasty cold after that dip in the river.

But it must be gone by now! You're playacting!
Meooowww!

You'll see! This will clear out your nose! I'm giving you a triple dose!
TCHOOF TCHOOF TCHOOF

ATCHOO!
ATCHOO!

Okay, let's go! Your sense of smell awakens while hunting!

Much later...
Well what? Still not the slightest trail?!
Sniff!

That's impossible, you're doing that deliberately! I think that even I smell...
SNIF SNIF

Yes, the scent is getting clearer... Ha! Ha! I have a better sense of smell than you!
SNIF SNIF SNIF
?

There! That little shadow that's moving... A Smurf!

TALLYHO!
37

Oh, sorry! That... that was a mistake!
Grumpf?

I SAID I'M SORRY!
GROAAAAR

Drat! He's not going to let us go!
GRRRRR

I... I think we finally lost him... I can't go on!
THUMPA
THUMPA
THUMPA

No, he's still there! We're doomed!
GROOO

Up here... ≻PFFF!≺... It's our last chance!

≻Whew!≺ He's leaving... That was a close call!

That bloodthirsty animal chased us halfway across the forest... I don't even know where I am anymore!

!!

38
No, I can't believe my eyes!
?

The Smurfs' village! Finally, after all these years!

Blessed be that good teddy bear!
BOING

No hesitating! Let's use the element of surprise!
FROUTCH

But... But... Where are all of them?!

Curses! I finally find their village, and they're gone!
?

These raspberries are smurfly good!
Two baskets all to ourselves! Yum!

Oh! Look out!
?

I swear, Azrael, I won't leave empty handed!
GARGAMEL!

We'll stay hidden here as long as it takes! They'll certainly end up coming back!

It's a catastrasmurf!
We have to go tell Papa Smurf!
39

Ah! Aaah! Good work, Handy Smurf! Now this is sport!

Now, let's get back fast and eat! I don't want to miss the beginning of the gazebo show.

?
Papa Smurf! Papa Smurf!
Something terrible has smurfed!

What?! Gargamel smurfed the path to the village?! How is that possible?
No idea! But he's not planning to smurf from there.
He decided to camp out in the woods until our return.

Now we're in a fine smurf! Luckily we're all safe here.

A tragedy would have smurfed without you, Handy Smurf.

Thanks to the Smurf and Turf Spa, our village was deserted when Gargamel found it.
WHAT? Gargamel has found our village?!

I wonder what nasty smurf was in there?
Me too! It was dissmurfing!
We eat badly... We sleep badly.... We're getting smurfed...
I think I won't smurf here much longer!
MENU
Smurf-stew Surprise

Gargamel has smurfed our village!
What?! No way!
40

Papa Smurf, it's awful!
Gargamel is at our home?
We have to smurf something!

DON'T PANIC!
Settle down!

It's true that Gargamel has found our village! But he's not going to destroy it! He's going to camp out there to smurf us all once we return!

One thing is certain: he won't come smurf us here! So, a little patience, we will find a way to chase him away!
But that huge brute is going to wreck our houses!
Smurfing his stupid big feet in my vegetable garden!
Eating our food!
Smurfing in our river!
We have to smurf him out of our home!

Tomorrow, I'll go see for myself! We can't smurf anything for the moment!

We have to smurf the show as planned in order to distract them!
I'll call Jokey Smurf.

Let's laugh a little! This is the story of the Smurf who went to smurf hazelnuts and, when he returned to the village--

To the village... Oooh, our beautiful village! *Sniff!*

Waaaah! I want to go home!
WAAAAAH!
Boo-hoo hoooo!
Us too! *WAAAAAH!*
Sniff!
41

Let's see... What else is in this attic?

Hmmm... Hazelnut spread! Delicious!
SLURP

I love their little appetizers, but honestly, that won't feed a man.
BOP

I'd better go fishing for my main course.

So, Azrael, aren't we fine here outdoors?

Smurf us down a little farther away. He mustn't see us.

He's camping over here, Papa Smurf!
I hope he's already tired of smurfing outdoors!

I've got to say, Azrael, this stay out in nature is doing me a world of good.

He's nowhere near leaving! We'll have to smurf action!
You're right.

Let's come back with all the Smurfs, bows, arrows, and let's smurf him--
No, Hefty Smurf, we won't smurf anything by force.

He has to decide on his own to smurf away from here. But we're going to help him out a little...
42

These cherries are delicious... This place is a true earthly paradise.

GARGAMEL! GARGAMEL!
Huh? Who's talking to me?

Gargamel! Listen...
What?! The Smurfs!

YOU MUST GO HOME RIGHT AWAY, GARGAMEL!

Go home? No way! I'm just fine here.

GARGAMEL, YOUR HOME IS GOING TO BURN DOWN! FLAMES ARE SMURFING IN THE CHIMNEY!

Oh, no, that won't work! You won't get me with such a crude trick!

I don't care anyways about that rotten old shack!

Hmm... If it burns, I'll lose my spell books... My furniture... All my keepsakes...

My old doll... My wheeled broom... The little bed where mama would come tuck me in...
Sleep, sleep, my little wizard... Go to sleep and get a lizard!
43

We warned you, Gargamel! If you want to save your house, you must run!

I must go... But if I go, I won't find their village again!

I have an idea!

Ha! Ha! I'll drop cherries behind me... I'll come back by following the trail!

Where are we going, Papa Smurf?
To Gargamel's home! We have a bonfire to smurf!

That trail idea is awesome! Mama told me a story like that, but I always fell asleep before the end!

I'd better arrive soon or I'm going to run out of cherries!

Oh, no!

Papa Smurf didn't lie!

My firewood!
44

Sorry, Gargamel! You'll have to go look for some wood!
Cursed Smurfs! You pulled one over on me once again!

Heh! Heh! Heh!

Oh, they were trying to be cleverer than me... They'll be pretty surprised to see me come back!

There's the next one! Ah-Ha! It's working wonderfully!

Oh, no! Hide, Azrael!

It's that brute of a bear again... Let's let him go by!

But? What's he picking up there?!

YUM
CHOMP
CHOMP
GULP
SLURP

PTOOIE

My cherries! He's guzzling down my trail!

RHAAAAA! I'M GOING TO TURN YOU INTO A BEDSIDE RUG!
?
45

Papa Smurf, Gargamel emptied our storage!
We'll have to smurf new supplies before winter.

Go tell the Smurfs to come home right away! Vacation is over.

Stupid bear! I gave him a good thrashing!

Life soon resumes its normal course...
I've got it this time! I know what wasn't smurfing with my machine.
?

Ah, you're just in time! Go smurf me a bag of cherries.
Come on, Handy Smurf, the season is over.

On the other hand, if you could refashion it so it'll smurf hazelnuts from their shells...
?

Hmm... It'll be fall soon...
PLIC

No more Smurf and Turf Spa! And, because of Gargamel, our vacations have been smurfed short.
Meh, too much of a good thing is always smurf!
And besides, we can always smurf back there next year!

THE END

THE ADVENTURES OF
JOHAN AND PEEWIT

THE GOBLIN OF ROCKY WOOD

One morning, at the King's castle, the drawbridge has just been lowered, granting passage to Johan and his faithful steed.

Ah! There's Francis the woodman!... Goodness! He looks very gloomy!

Hello, Francis! Is something amiss?
Uh! Oh! No, Milord Johan.

Well, yes, in fact. Nothing's right since Peewit has been in the area.
Peewit?

Well, yes, Peewit. How come you don't know that demon's been haunting the Rocky Wood for some time now?
No! But what exactly is this Peewit?

Some say he's a goblin. Others say he's wicked fairy, but I'm sure he's Satan personified.
But what's he like? Have you seen him yet?

Yes! One day, I saw him in the woods. He was as tiny as this. But another time, a blacksmith saw him and he was this tall.

When Peewit saw me, he stopped and started making horrible faces at me!

Then, suddenly, pfffweet! He disappeared into thin air!

And then he passed right beside me, astride a diabolical animal that ran like the wind, and he was howling
PEEEEEEEWiiiT!
1

EEEEWiiiT

Did--did you hear? That's--that's him!
No, that's just the echo. Listen...

EEOOO OOO...

EEOOO OOO...
Well now. And I thought it was Peewit! HA HA HA! Peewit!

PEEEWiiiiT!

FRANCIS...

Man or demon? I have to be sure!
Uh, wait for me!

There! Something moved in that underbrush.

SHUFF SHUFF

HERE, FRANCIS! I GOT HIM!

Peyo
2

You--you got him?
No! He must have fled farther away!

Just say he disappeared. You can't catch Peewit.

If that demon keeps playing tricks on me, I'll go see the King.
If it's a demon, you should go see the monks at the abbey. All right, see you soon.

Now, to work. Hey! I'd have sworn there was a bush here earlier.

Why... what's going on? I can't lift my ax now?

Peewit! I'd like to meet that jokester.

Ah! Milord Johan! I was just looking for you. The King's asking for you.
All right. Let's go.

PEEEWiiiiT!

Oh, my! What's--

Hearing that cry, I hurried to see a demon grimacing in my orchard!

By the time I got my shoes on, he'd disappeared! With my loveliest apples!

That's the first time I've ever heard of a demon having fun stealing apples.

Hello, friar. Is the King there?
Yes. He's awaiting you. Go in.

Ah! There you are, Johan! Come, I have to speak to you!

A messenger arrived this morning. He brought me a parchment telling me Princess Anne, my niece, is coming to spend a few days at the castle.

I'd like you to attend to her stay here. Have her room brightened up, organize a tournament in her honor, and ask the troubadours to come entertain her. I'm counting on you for everything to be nice.

I'll do my best, Sire.
Good! That done, I have another mission to entrust to you.

It's about that Peewit...
!
Peyo
4

Have you heard about him?
Oh! Yes, Sire! This morning, I even witnessed one his tricks.

Oh, yes? Unfortunately, he's not content just playing tricks on people. He scaring them and stealing their apples... and their pâtés! Good pâté that was meant for me, blast it!

I want my people to live in peace and security! I'm trusting you to set things right. Speaking of which, what's that Peewit like? Have you see him?

No, sire! But according to what I've heard, he's a hideous, evil monster, a wicked genie, a gnome, a sorcerer, and demon all at once!

Uh... Oh, yeah?! Hmm! Ha ha! We-we do know there's no such thing as that! All right, go now!

And...uh! Be careful, nevertheless. You never know.

A few moments later...

It's no use! That infernal Peewit refuses to show his face.

You just wait, my friend! I have what I need here to bring you out of hiding.
Peyo 5

Milord Peewit, it's just you and me.

First: Some dry moss, a little wood, and I make a nice fire.

Second: A few leaves... →pfff!←... on them to... →pfff!←... signal my... →pfff!←... presence to him.
FFFSSSSS

So much smoke! Third: Let's bring out the bait...

A superb, big, fat chicken, just asking to be eaten... by Peewit!

Cooked to perfection. Now I just have to outwit him.

I'll pretend to look for some wood.

I go away a little.

Once I'm far enough not to be seen...

I'll return quietly, hide in a thicket, and when he comes to steal my chicken, I'll--

?
?

PEEEWiiiiiT!
6 Peyo

My chicken! That scoundrel! Luckily he can't be far!

There he is! Hey! But... he's a dwarf?!

?

So, Milord Peewit, you like chicken from what I see. Come here, I have a few things to tell you.

BOOOOOooo!...

Wait! Where did he go?

WAAAA!

Dir-- dirty kid! If I ever catch you, I'll--

WAAAA!

Just you wait, scamp! If I have to tear out every blade of grass, I'll get you!

?

I got you this time!
!!

Ah ha! You're losing ground, mister!

?
ANNIE!

ANNIE...
?!

ANN--

No more jokes, Peewit!
Peyo
8

BOP
ANNIE!

HA HA HA HA! Let's go, my beauty! Down with the enemy!

Zounds! Where'd that animal come from? It's charging again!

All right, no kidding around. This little game can't go on forever. Careful.

POW
BAM

Oww, my head! ANNIE! An-Annie!

It's nothing! She's just stunned! You see? She's already opening her eyes.

You know, I'm sorry for stealing your chicken, because you're nice to Annie, despite everything she and I did to you. You're not mad at us?

Of course not. But don't start again.
I swear!

BOP
Peyo
9

?
Annie! I've told you a hundred times not to head-butt people without me telling you to! Go on, get! Come back when I call you.

All right! Now, listen closely, Peewit. You're all they're talking about around here!

And, unfortunately, not good things! The serfs have come to complain at the castle, and the tales of your thefts have greatly displeased the King.

One day, exasperated, they'll form a hunting party, capture you, and then--
Oh! They won't catch me, not even if there were a hundred of them.

And why not? I caught you all by myself!
!

But, tell me, you haven't always lived here? What did you do before?
I was going from farm to farm seeking work, but everywhere people mocked me and chased me away.

I've been wandering the roads for a long time, my stomach empty. Till one day, while crossing these woods, I met a man who, upon seeing me, ran away, shouting: "A goblin! There's a goblin in the Rocky Wood!" So, I got the idea to pass myself off as a real goblin! And since then, I've been living peacefully here.

Yes! Until the day when people have had enough of seeing their apples and pâtés disappear! No, believe me, you should do something else.

I wish! But what?
Waitaminute! Why not... at the castle?

Of course! And why not? Peewit, you'll be the King's jester!
?!
Peyo
10

The King's jester? Me? Oh, that would be marvelous! And look what all I can do!

Tumbling! Cartwheels! Walking on my hands!

An assortment of grimaces that range from scary to funny!

I know several legends, I'm pretty quick-witted, and what's more, I have a rather pretty voice! Listen... -Ahem!-...

A JUGGLER ON THE VIOL AM I A FRIEND OF MUSE AND SKY,
!

AND THOUGH JUMPING LIKE YE GOAT, WELL I SING EVERY NOTE.

Magnificent! I'll go back to the castle, talk to the King about it and, if he agrees, come look for you tomorrow morning!

A little later at the castle...
TOK TOK

Ah! It's you, Johan. Don't make any noise. The King is ill!
Ill?! Is it serious?

No! He'll be back on his feet in a few days. I had him take a calming potion, and now he's sleeping.

Ah! While I'm thinking about it, the King said to tell you to not forget about Princess Anne's arrival.
No, no! He can count on me.

Poor King! This really isn't the time to talk to about Peewit.

The next morning...
You understand, I really couldn't wake him to talk about you.
Of course not.
Peyo
11

In a few days, he'll be better. In the meantime, try to lay low. Keep very quiet and, above all, no stealing!

But... what will I eat then?
I brought you a few supplies! Come!

Here! There's ham, chicken, eggs, and a cabbage for Annie!
?

Look, Annie! See what Johan brought you?
Hey! Where did she come from?

Uh... yes, all right! All right! Good girl!
That's it! She's adopted you now!

Very well! I'll return to the castle. Once there's anything new, I'll come let you know. See you soon!
See you soon! Thanks!

Three days passed. And that morning...
How's the King today?
Much better.

I'm happy to see you cured, sire. Everything is ready for Princess Anne's arrival.

That's very good, Johan. And what became of that Peewit? Have the serfs come again to complain about him?
Now's the time!

No! I think he's changed his ways. And I even propose that you take him--

SIRE! SIRE! COME QUICKLY! PRINCESS ANNE HAS BEEN ABDUCTED!
!

What... what are you saying? Abducted? But-but that's impossible! Who told you that?
Two soldiers from her escort who just arrived at the castle.

Abducted! Abducted by whom? And why?

Where did it happen? Where is she? Speak, I tell you!

So it was like this... We'd made the trip without any incident and, this morning, we were crossing the Rocky Wood when, suddenly, we were attacked by a goblin of awesome might! In an instant we were thrown to the ground, stunned, and tied up! Right, Angelot?
Yes, Philibert!
?

Only Angelot and I managed to escape! And while running, we heard the goblin howling.

I can still hear it howling: PEEWIT! PEEWIT!
??!

PEEWIT! So it's him! That brigand! That-that
But, sire, it's not-

SADDLE UP, EVERYONE! A THOUSAND CROWNS TO WHOEVER RESCUES THE PRINCESS AND BRINGS BACK PEEWIT DEAD OR ALIVE!

What's this all about? Peewit doesn't have awesome strength. And why would he have abducted the princess? I don't get it!

Peyo
13

But Peewit seemed sincere. Could he have lied to me and to what end?

And what if the others catch him before me? They'll kill him, and I'd never learn the truth.

Gallop, old friend! I must arrive before they do.

!?
!

Ah! There he is!

Quick! Hop on!
?

But... what's going on?

We're far enough away! They won't come looking for you here.
Looking for me? Who is? And why?

Why? Because this morning, Princess Anne was abducted and two soldiers from her escort managed to escape and accuse you of being responsible for that attack.
ME?

But that's not true! And I can prove it because I know who attacked the princess and her escort.
Peyo 14

What are you saying? You know who Princess Anne's assailants are? But how?

This morning, I was perched in a tree when I saw twenty or so scoundrels come and hide in the underbrush. Soon after, a small group of riders and a few carts came along. At a signal, the bandits rushed at them. The less numerous riders were disarmed and bound. The princess they were escorting was taken prisoner too.

So two of the attackers exchanged clothes with their captives and left in the direction of the castle. They're the ones who accused me, no doubt?
Yes!

I'll see them hanged! I'll go to the castle and tell the King the truth!
And he won't believe you because there's no proof they were part of the attackers. And you'll be the one getting hanged.

What we must learn is who abducted the princess! Listen, here's what we're going to do! Tonight... ... ...
... ...

Later...
We've searched the entire forest, bush by bush, and nothing. Not the slightest trace of Peewit or of the princess...

Poor girl! Well, resume the search tomorrow. At dawn, gentlemen, I'm counting on you.

Night is falling! I think it's time to set my plan into motion.

Have the drawbridge lowered.

Peyo
15

Where's he going?
I don't know! Maybe--Hey, Look! He's already coming back. He must have forgotten something!

You can have the drawbridge raised again. Good night!
?
?

Hey! Keep still!

Careful! Someone's coming!

Good evening!
Uh! Good evening!

Whew! I think he didn't see anything.

All right! We're here.

And now, listen closely. You're going to hide in the room of the two scoundrels who accused you. You'll listen to what they say and, with a little luck, perhaps we can learn something. Furthermore, I'll be sure to make them talkative.

Wait for me here. I'll go see if we can go in there.
Uh, yes, yes. Take your time, I'm in no hurry.

All's clear! They're still eating in the great room. Come!
Already?

It's here! Is this all right? You're not afraid?
N--n--no, no!

Heavens! There they are! Just in time.
Peyo 16

Ah! Gentlemen, I was looking for you. Wouldn't you like a jug of wine before you go to bed?
Heh heh! That's an excellent idea! Run, grab us one. And your best wine!

Here you are! If you want any more, just ask me for some. Good night.

Do you believe it, Angelot? What a princely life! Ha ha ha! If they knew we were in the employ of--
Shh! Shut up, Philibert! Someone may be listening to us.

Hmm! That's right! Wait! I'll go see if there's anyone in the hallway!

No, we're good. Say, this little wine here-- →hic!←--isn't bad!
Not bad at all!

Phi Philibert! Look! There's... there's... no more wine!

No more? Ohhh, →hic!← No problem! I'll go ask for-- →hic!←... Pee.... A... A... What's his name again? Peewit? Ah, no!
→Hic!←

No, that's the little idiot who-- →hic!←... supposedly attacked us! Ha ha ha! →Hic!←

RRIP

Philibert! Hey! Phil-- →hic!←... bert! My word, he's sleeping! Oh! And I'm goning-- →hic!← ...do likewise! If I keep on drinking, I'll end up-- →hic!← ...drunk!
ZZZZzz zzz

ZZZZzzz ZZzz
ZZZZZ ZZZ
Peyo 17

CREEEEEEEEEEE
ZZZzz
zz

That was really worth spending my time here not finding out anything and getting called a little idiot!

Little idiot! Little idiot! Repeat that if you dare, you fat pile of snoring lard! If you think I'm scared of you!
ZZZzz
zz

Take that, you--
ZZzz --Huh? NO!

No! Mercy! It's not me!

I'm innocent! Girard of Waltriquet's the one who abducted the princess! Mercy! ->Boohooooo!<-
Why, he's dreaming.

Heh heh! I think this will interest Johan! Goodnight, wine-bag!

Girard of Waltriquet! So, he's responsible for that attack.
You must tell the King! He'll besiege Waltriquet and rescue the princess!

That's impossible! Let's say the King were to believe me. Even before he comes within sight of Waltriquet's towers, Girard would be alerted. He'd have put the princess in safekeeping and, once the King arrives, he'd find nothing!

We must have proof in order to convince the King and we'll go find it at Waltriquet's. Peewit, we're leaving before dawn tomorrow!
!!

The next morning...
Peyo
18

Hup! All right! You can come out!
Oww!
Johan! There's a rider behind us!
?!

Whew!
None too soon! I was smothering in there!

All right! Let's go!

Who could it be? Let's hide and let him pass by.

There he is! But but that's the Knight Piefroy!

What's he doing out here? Well, no matter! Let's go!

Is it far still?
No! We're almost there!

Peyo
19

How will we-- hey, somebody's leaving the castle! Why, it's Piefroy!

Wait for me here!

Hello, milord! Having a ride?
!?

Uh, yes... no, I-I was looking for Peewit!
My, my! And you were looking for him inside Waltriquet's castle?

What... no! Why?
Because I saw you coming out of that castle and I strongly suspect you of having helped Girard to adbd--

I don't have time to waste listening to your balderdash! Let me by, or else--!
NO!
Not till you've told me what you were doing at Waltriquet's!

It's none of your business! Back, confound you!

Peyo
20

ZZZZWIP
ZZZZ

HEY! LOOK--

POW
BAM

WHUUHHH!

Now, talk! Admit that you helped Waltriquet to abduct Princess Anne! Where is she?

In my castle, Milord Johan!
?!

Girard of Waltriquet!
And I'll be very happy to offer you my hospitality there! Heh heh heh! The best cell will be at your disposal!
Peyo
21

All right! Get going!

Well, now I'm in an awful fix! How will I get out of this? And Peewit's waiting for me!

!!?

Good heavens! Johan's been captured! And Piefroy's laughing with the fat bearded one! But then... that redhead is a traitor!

There's no way I'm rotting in here! How can I escape?

It's no use! This door is solid. And there's surely a guard on the other side, I wouldn't get far.

HMMMF!
No! There's no way to loosen this bar!

But I must get out of here! Or alert the King that I'm Waltriquet's prisoner! If only I could see Peewit!

Hmm, there goes that felon Piefroy leaving the castle! I can't stop him this time!

What if I stunned my guard? Or tried to bribe him? Or if I pretended to be dead?
Peyo
22

While Johan's seeking a way to escape, Piefroy takes the road to the King's castle again...

BOP

You weren't expecting that, were you, you filthy traitor!

-Oof!- What a big, fat lump! But I got to hide him in the bushes!

There! That's done with! Now, I have to find some way to rescue Johan!

Hey! What's that coming along there? Aha, a hay cart! That's some unexpected luck!

A little later...
So, right when the jailor brings me food, I'll jump him, knock him out, and run. It's risky, but it's my only chance!

Here goes! There he is! One... two...
CRIC CRAC

Follow me. Milord Girard wants to talk to you.
Thr--!?!
Peyo
23

*See SMURFS AND FRIENDS, vol. 1

You weren't expecting to see me again here, were you? And how is Milord of Basenhau? Still in the King's prisons?
Still! He's waiting for you to join him! Which will be soon enough!

I doubt that! Heh heh! I haven't done anything. Peewit's the one who abducted the princess!
Exactly! Peewit will call you to account one day!

Ha ha ha! Let him come! We'll give him a warm welcome!
Ha ha ha ha!

PEEEWiiiiT!

What-what scoundrel's having fun--

Well? What's going on? Who let out that cry?
A-a goblin, Milord!

He was hiding in a hay cart! We tried to capture him, but he slipped between our legs and disappeared. Then we heard it howl: "PEEEWiiiiT!" But when we got to where the cry was coming from, there was nobody there! It's-- it's the devil, Milord!

THE DEVIL! THE DEVIL! What's that poppycock? Catch me that Peewit... and fast!

Jailor, take Johan back to his prison! And... chain him up, that's more prudent!

PEEEWiiiiT!
Brave Peewit! I hope he doesn't get caught!
25

There's something I don't understand. If Peewit is here, it's because he knows I'm the one who accused him... How did he find out? A mystery! Anyhow, we must prevent him from leaving the castle at all costs.

There's no way that fat brute is clapping me in irons. I'd have no further chance of escape.

There he is! Too bad, I'll go for broke!
CRIC CRAC

?!

PEEWIT! Stop laughing like that, you'll rouse the whole castle!
HA! HA! HA!

Look out! Someone is coming this way!

Where the devil could that Peewit be hiding?

HUH?! HELP--

One peep, one move, and you're a dead man! Where is Princess Anne? Answer!
The... the.... cell be-beside the jailor's storeroom! The door on the le-left!

Anybody?
Nope! Let's go!

Faster, Peewit! There's not a moment to lose!
Peyo 27

It must be here!

=Hhhnn!= It's no use. We have to find the key to this lock!
I saw a whole bunch at the jailor's!

=Buhh!=... What... Oh! My head!
Look out!

Hey there! Behave!
BOP

Is that it?
Yes! Here goes!

Courage, Princess! We're here-- ?!
?

We were tricked! There's only that poor old man in the cell on the right!
On the right? But... but the soldier said the one on the left!

For mercy's sake! Couldn't you have said so sooner?

Blast it! I can't find the right key!
Johan, hu-hurry up! I hear footsteps!
28
Peyo

At last!
Quick! Quick!

Come quickly, Princess! Waltriquet's men are coming! Hurry!

Yikes! There they are!

He's managed to rescue Johan and the princess!

Go on! I'll see to stopping them!
!

PEEEEWiiiT!

We've got them. This hallway is a dead end!

PEEEEWiiiT!

There! They're trying to escape through the chimney!
29 Peyo

ZOUNDS!
It's only Peewit! The others are gone!

Capture him, you two! We'll pursue Johan and the princess!

Good! My plan worked! Now I have to get rid of those two!

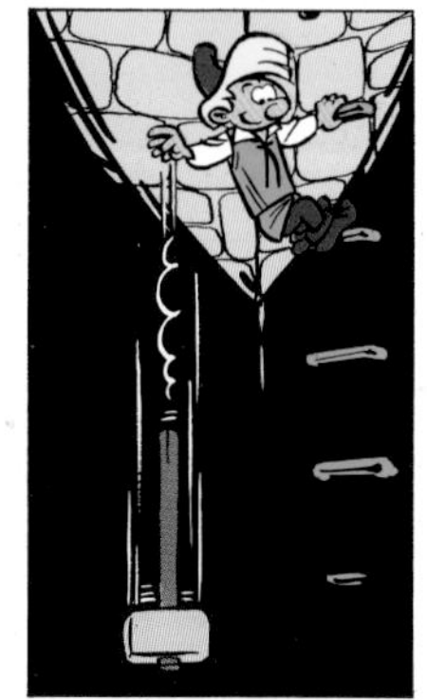

BROUMBLIGLONG
BING
PANG

Oh, my!

How will I get down from here?

Meanwhile...
Peewit must have succeeded. They're no longer pursuing us!

I hope-- HEY! Be careful, Princess!
?

Listen! There's fighting up there!
Peyo
30

I don't hear anything now. They must be captured.
No doubt!

?
?*☆!@*
GET MOVING!
They can't be far!

Look out! Another one! Try to get closer to the drawbridge!

There's Johan and the princess! Hey! Is that guard going to stop them? No! Johan took him down! Yikes! There are two more!

CLANG

THERE THEY ARE! WE'VE GOT THEM!

Aie yai yai! And even more! For crying out loud, Johan will fall to their numbers!

If only I could--
HEEEY--

Surrender, Johan!

?
?
PAF

Johan! Quick, this way! This door is open!
31

POC

TAC
SLAM

Johan! I...I can't go on!
Courage, Princess! We must go on! It's our only chance!

Faster! Faster!

Close the trapdoor!

BAM
!
?!

Get up, by the devil! Let's break through that trapdoor!

BOOM
BAM

Whew! It sounds like they're giving up! Let's take this chance to set this beam solidly!

There! Ah? Has Peewit awakened? Ho there, Peewit! How do you feel?
Uhhhhh?! Where... where am I?

Well? Do you have them?
Uh, no! They've barricaded themselves atop the tower.
Peyo
32

WHAT?
AND THAT'S WHAT'S STOPPING YOU?

THEN GET THE BATTERING RAMS, DEMOLISH THE TOWER, OR SET IT ON FIRE, IF NECESSARY!
Wait, Milord!

In fact, they're prisoners in that tower! Let's keep an eye on the door and windows until, driven by hunger and thirst, they're forced to surrender.
Hmm. You may be right.

We mustn't fool ourselves. We're far from safe! And what's worse is that traitor Piefroy went to lay a trap for the King! And tomorrow, the King will be Waltriquet's prisoner!
Oh! I don't think so!

No! He won't because I left Piefroy tied up and gagged in a bush...

Well done! Good job, Peewit! In that case, we just have to find some way to get out of here.

Whew!
It won't be easy. We'd need ropes.

Johan! There are old clothes in this chest. Maybe we could tear them apart and tie the pieces end to end?
All right, but let's hurry. Night will fall soon.

Later...
There! I hope that'll be solid enough. Now, listen to me closely.

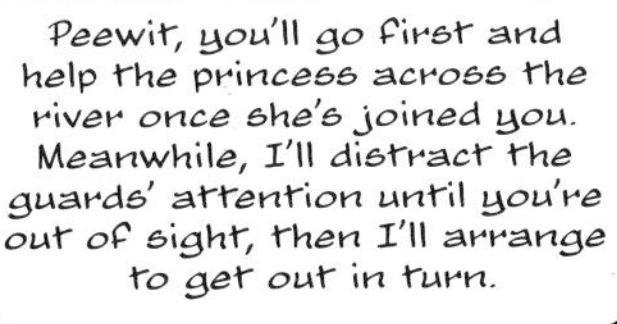
Peewit, you'll go first and help the princess across the river once she's joined you. Meanwhile, I'll distract the guards' attention until you're out of sight, then I'll arrange to get out in turn.

Here goes! Are you ready? Go ahead, Peewit!
Peyo 33

TOOOOO

TOO TOOOOOOO
?
?
?

TOOOOOOOOOO

What's going on? Who's sounding a horn?
It's Johan, Milord! Look! You can see him from here!

TOOTOOTOOOOO
What's gotten into him? Loose a few arrows to shut him up!
?!

LOOK OUT! It's a trick! There's one trying to get away!

ALERT THE OTHER GUARDS! SHOOT HIM DOWN!
WWIIIIT

Johan! Johan! They've seen Peewit! They're shooting at him!

Good heavens, he'd better jump in the river or he's done for! JUMP, PEEWIT!

Ju-jump? I'll bust my head again! No way!
WWIIIIIT

RIP
HEY!

KRESH

PLOOOSH
Peyo
34

He's not coming up! Ha ha ha! This time, I think he's done for! We can go to bed.
Yes! Keep watching the tower, you others.
Johan, it's awful! Do you think he's....?
Alas! I don't have much hope.
NO! There! He's climbing the bank! He swam underwater to there!
I hope they don't see him. No! That's it! He's out of sight now!
->Whew!<- I thought I was a goner! Meanwhile, Johan and the princess now have no other chance to escape. There's only one solution: go alert the King!
I hope he'll want to listen to me. It won't be easy, especially if he still believes I'm the one who abducted the princess.
Hey! That's the place where I left that traitor Piefroy. Let's see if I'd better retighten his bonds.
Hello?! I'd have sworn here was where-- Hey! What--?
ZOUNDS! The scoundrel managed to free himself!
But... but... but then, he's at the King's castle! What a disaster! All is lost!
Peyo 35

I have to get to the castle before the King departs!

With the first glimmer of dawn, Peewit arrives in sight of the Rocky Wood...
I pray Annie is there! I can't go on!

Annie!
ANNIE!

Ah! My Annie!

?
Get going! We're going to the castle, old friend! Hurry!

Faster, Annie! Faster!

Whoa there! What the--?
HALT!

POW

SIRE! DON'T LEAVE! IT'S A TRAP!
36

Piefroy is in the service of those who abducted Princess Anne! He was going to lead you into an ambush!
That's false! And I--

But after all, what proof do I have that you're telling me the truth?
It's simple! Piefroy said you should pay Peewit a ransom, didn't he? Well, that's false!

And if I dare say so, Peewit is ME!

Zounds! Torture that traitor Piefroy until he tells us who abducted the princess and where she is!
There's no need, Sire! Give me a bellyful first and I'll tell you everything that's happened.

So it was Waltriquet who engineered this whole affair! And yet, those two soldiers from the princess's escort, who told me you were the one who attacked them...
...are Waltriquet's men! Moreover, I have an idea to confound them! Listen... ... ...

Someone wants to talk to us? Oh?! Fine! We're coming!

Ah! There you are! Waltriquet sent me! He wants to know if everything has gone well and if anyone suspects anything.

Suspect anything? Ha ha! There's no danger! That doddering, old King is more convinced than ever that a certain Peewit has abducted the princess! Right, Angelot?
Yes, Philibert!

Tell Waltriquet he can rest easy and that the old coot is ripe for falling into Piefroy's trap.

Do you understand anything, Angelot?
No, Philibert!
Idiots!
37

Later, at Girard of Waltriquet's castle...
Well, what's Piefroy doing? He should have been here with the King long ago!
Patience, Milord. They won't be long.

MI-MILORD! THE KING IS HERE! AT THE CASTLE GATES!
Ah! Finally! Bring him to me!

WHAT?
He-he's here with his whole army!

Hurrah! Look, princess, we're saved! The King's coming to besiege the castle! And Peewit is at his side! Brave little fellow!

There they are, Sire! Do you see them? They're waving their arms!
Yes! PREPARE FOR THE ASSAULT!

That dirty, little scamp Peewit wasn't dead! Quick, we must organize the castle's defense before they attack!
Peyo
38

They're too numerous. We won't hold out for long! Let's capture the princess and Johan and, with those hostages, victory is ours!
Hmm. Yes. Maybe.

That's it! They've managed to set a ladder! Look out! They're going to--
JOHAN!

YIKES!
CRAC

Try to surprise them from outside! And careful, I need them alive!

William!
You to ?!?
Well? Where did he go?

The first one to poke his head in-- what?
LOOK!

WAM

This time, no retreat is possible! We're doomed!
Peyo 39

Hurry up, blast it! The King's men are already on the ramparts!

HOLD ON, JOHAN!

WAC

The tide has turned, Waltriquet! I'm picturing you with a nice hemp collar around your neck!

Ha ha! Take that!

BOP

Come on, Waltriquet, resistance is futile! Surrender!

Well! Now you're more reasonable! And William? Where is he? Why isn't he with you?
I don't know! He disappeared as the assault began. I bet he's cowardly abandoned me and fled through the tunnels!

Evidently! When that coward saw things were turning for the worse, he hurried to get away! You others, lead the princess to safety! Peewit and I will try to catch William!

Let's go, Peewit!
Peyo
40

He has a serious lead on us! We'll be lucky to overtake him!

Ho there, scoundrel! Did you see William come this way? Speak or else!

Uh! Y-yes! He left through the tunnel! There, behind that slab! He said he was going for reinforcements!
Reinforcements? Ah, right! That's good, go away!

That's it, here's the passage. Let's go!

Here's the way out of the tunnel!
And none too soon! I was starting to think it'd never end!

Whew! Now, where is William?

There! That's him! Blast it! How did he manage to find a horse?

We must return to the castle! That's the only way to get myself a horse!

Quick, rider, give me your horse!
?
ANNIE!
41

There he is!

I'm being pursued! Why, it's Johan! So Waltriquet didn't succeed. I have to be rid of him once and for all.

Heh heh! Some unexpected luck!

This is good! This rock will topple easily! Ha! I hear them!

Well, I never! His horse!? And where is he?
?

HHNN!
And there! Farewell, Milord Johan!

BROOM
LOOK OUT!

WOOM

All right, you wicked crow, come down from your perch! There's a nice cage waiting for you!

T-tie up that filthy beast, first! Tie it up!

Meanwhile, the King's soldiers have taken control of Waltriquet's castle. A total victory!

A few days later, while William and Waltriquet meditate in dark cells, Johan and Princess Anne tell their adventures to the King...

That sounds like Peewit's voice! What's going on?
?

Ah! There you are! Farewell! I'm leaving!

You're leaving? But why? Just yesterday, you were telling me that--
Yes! But something's happened since then! I've been injured!
Oh, no! Is it serious? Where are you injured?
In my dignity!

Come now, think, Peewit! You have the luck to be named the King's jester, you're housed, fed, and dressed.
Dressed! Ah, well, yes! Let's talk about that. I thought being a jester meant being funny but without being ridiculous for all that. Ha ha ha! What a mistake!

But come now...
What's more, you can judge for yourself! Wait for me here. I'll be right back!

I don't understand a thing. Do you, Sire?
Me neither! And the strange thing is that he hasn't even spoken to me about the surprise I sent to him earlier!
Johan! He's not leaving, is he?

No, Princess! Ah! There he is!
I'm warning you, if any of you dares to laugh, I-I'll hit the roof!
DING
DING
DING

Ah! Why, that's my surprise!
Well! What a surprise! I'm happy to stay, but I refuse to wear this... this costume
DING
TING
DING
DING
44

THE END

DING
DING
TINC
DING

SPELLS AT THE CASTLE

They're asleep, too! -Sniff!- ...but they don't smell like wine. Peewit, we must immediately alert the King.

The seneschal! Good heavens, it's an epidemic!
But, when we left this morning, everything was normal!
ZZZZZZZ

He's not answering! Too bad, let's go in!
KNOCK
KNOCK

Sire! **SIRE!** Him, too?!

It's impossible! Someone must have cast a spell on the castle!
M-m-maybe... it's a wi-wicked witch?...

What about that quack who came yesterday, offering the King all sorts of magical remedies? He had a wicked look to him!
Both of his eyes looked evil to me.

You think he's still here?
We'll go see!

There he is, but he's asleep, too!
So that evil spell isn't from him! But from whom then?
ZZZZZ... ZZZZ

Hey, you're not asleep! And you're hungry? Wait!
Woof! Woof!

Here, eat up, big guy!
GULP
LAP

Let's search the castle from top to bottom! We must find the source of this sinister joke! He surely hasn't fallen asleep!

!?
ZZZZZZZ
2

There's the explanation! Someone has put a drug in the food! We just have to find out who. Let's go see in the kitchens!

Above all, don't taste anything!
Aww!... That'll be hard!

That's it! I think I've found it! Smell this!...
PEE-YEW!

But why would someone drug the whole castle?
To be able to pillage it at his leisure, no doubt! Our arrival must have caught him by surprise and he's hiding. Let's pretend to sleep like the others...

GOOD HEAVENS! Why didn't I think of that earlier?
Huh? What's gotten into you?

That's right! That scoundrel was pretending to sleep!

We must stop him from leaving the castle. Come help me raise the drawbridge!

HELLO?
CLING
CLING

Why, it's the traveling salesman from earlier.
Lower the drawbridge!

Now I understand why he didn't sell us anything. He's an accomplice of the charlatan and he's coming to take delivery of the castle's goods. Their little trick isn't bad, is it? Here, hand me the guard's bow and arrows!

?!
SPOC

Hee hee hee! I think he understood that! Did you see how he ran?
Now we have to capture our drug merchant!
ZZZZZ

TAP
TAP
TAP
Listen! Someone's walking in the upstairs room! It's him! Let's go!

There's no use playing the sleepwalker, mister! You fooled us once, not twice!

31

Goodness, he really does seem to be asleep!
You think? He knows he's caught and is risking it all!

Hello! Lower the drawbridge!
Him again?! Watch this one. I'll go have a word with him.

Open up! I must see the King!

See the king?... See what's in his coffers, you mean!... Hey, that one is waking up...
Buhh?

That's it! The drug has lost its effect. Come along, everyone, Peewit and I have the one who put you to sleep.
?
?

Sire, that quack is the one who drugged you all. No doubt to be able to rob you at his leisure!
Huh? But that's false! I swear to you I'm innocent!

A traveling salesman is asking to see the King.
What? My, what nerve! Bring him here, but under close guard. That's his accomplice!

But-but let me go! I'm an honest merchant!

Ah! Sire, I beg your pardon! Mercy, Sire!
So you admit it then, churl?

Yes, sire! I admit mistaking the flask! Instead of the herbal juice, this morning, I sold your cook a sleeping potion meant for the Duke of Dordeboux! After I realized my error, I immediately came back to warn you! Alas, it seems I was too late. Mercy, Sire, mercy!
!!

They can attack the castle, pillage it, set it on fire, if they like. I'm not budging!
?
Peyo
41

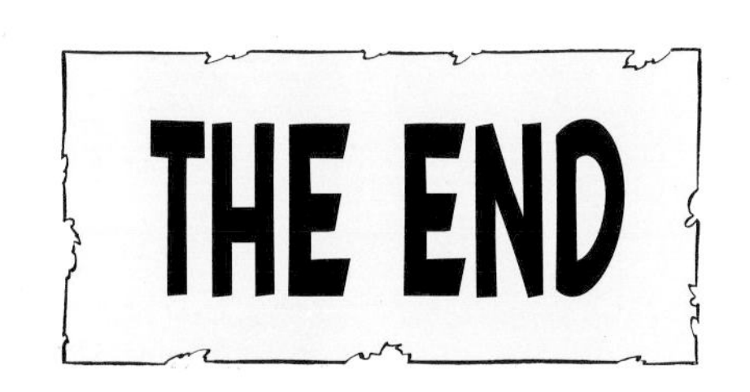

THE END

ENGUERRAN THE VALIANT

Peyo

→Whew!← I thought he'd never stop recounting his exploits. I wonder how much of what he says is true? I'd like to see him at work.
Yes, me too! Heh heh! I think I have a little idea!
The next morning...
Enguerran! I have to ride three hours from here. Will you accompany me?
Gladly! I'll take this chance to tell you how, one day, I put a hoard of looters to flight...
Do you have your sword? The roads aren't safe that way. You sometimes have some unhappy encounters.
Oh?!...
We could take that shortcut through the woods. Alone, I wouldn't dare venture there, but with you, I fear nothing....
Uh, clearly!...
So? Your story about looters?
Huh?... Ah! Yes! Don't...don't you feel like we're being watched?...
EEEWEET
Hey? What was that?
Get them!
?
HUH!?
Quick! Unsheathe your sword, Enguerran! There's only ten of them!
Hang in there, Johan, I'll go get help!
2

Yikes! A marsh! I'm doomed!
PLITCH
PLATCH

HELP! I can't swim! I'll drown!

Enguerran!? But...you're a prisoner? That's impossible!
Uh...yes! I don't understand it myself. It's the first time that's happened to me.

Go on laughing, you big cowards, Enguerran would make short work of any one of you.
Uh... you shouldn't exaggerate!

Ah? Yes? Heh heh heh! Pipsqueak, come here!

Pipsqueak, this handsome whippersnapper wants to fight one of us. May as well be you as any other...

Ha ha ha! That's your champion? ⇾Pffff!⇽... he's brought down tougher ones! Haven't you, Enguerran?
Y-yes! Of-- of course!

Go ahead, make him eat dust!

S-s-stop! I'm-I'm suffocating! I--I give up!

Well what? He was unlucky, that's all! But give him his sword and you'll see what he can he do!
Fine! We'll give him back his sword, a coat of mail, and a shield. I'll take the challenge.
3

Are you ready?
Y-yes!

You'll see! This won't last long!
Ha ha ha! Right! It's already over!
PANG
TZING

Ho ho ho! Your Enguerran would do better to play with a rattle than with a sword!

A rattle? Come now, one day he stood up to ten men a lot bigger than you...and he was wounded! You can all attack him at once, and he'll beat you!

NO!
It's not true! I've never defeated anyone! I invented all those stories because I was afraid of seeming like a coward!

Ah! Finally! Hey, Robert, untie me!

Yes! We're free, Enguerran! These brigands are only the King's faithful servants. We wanted to see if you were as valiant as you were saying! Hmm... a future knight must be modest, Enguerran. Leave it to troubadours to sing of your exploits... once you've accomplished them.

Yes! Yes, you're right, Johan. I won't forget it. Alas! I must leave the castle now. I'll be everyone's laughingstock.

No! We promise you to never speak of what happened.
I swear!
I promise!
My word!

A few days later...
Have you seen the two bandits who were just brought in?
Yes! They remind me of those I was pursuing one day. I was going to catch them when, suddenly, they turned and attacked me.

Ahem...

Uh, Sire, believe me if you like, but I ran away!
THE END

THE SMURFS GAGS

120 SMURF JOKES

Stupid potion! It always smurfs up in my face!

I'm going to ask Papa Smurf's advice. He has lots of experience.
NOK NOK NOK

Stupid potion!
NO SMURFING
423

HELP, Hefty Smurf! There's a huge spider in my home!
Have no fear, Smurfette! I'm here!

What's great about Smurfette is that there's always some way to show off. The tiniest thing scares her.

Don't you worry! I'll smurf your monster out quick!
169

Hefty Smurf, I'll bet you two hazelnuts you can't stay on my ride two seconds.
Deal!
CLAP

Come here, Hedgy!
103

Thanks, Dopey Smurf, that was very pretty, but Smurfette's house is a little farther along!
© Peyo

I bet you a raspberry drink I can put out that candle with this remote I invented.
Deal!

© Peyo - 2002 Lic. IMPS (Brussels)
POP

I'll take it with ice!
550

That's weird. I have the uncomfortable feeling of being followed by a few smurfs...

!?
KIK
© Peyo - 2003 Lic. IMPS (Brussels)

?!?
Hee! Hee! Hee! This invisibility potion of Papa Smurf's is wonderful! I wonder if he has a little left...
623

Hey, Painter Smurf, could you smurf my portrait?
Uh... wouldn't you prefer a landscape?

I'm fed up with smurfing portraits.
439

Uh... I think your new golf course is a little different, Handy Smurf.
Well, it was the only way Clumsy Smurf could still smurf a few balls in the smurfs, Papa Smurf.
285

I've smurfed a cake that deserves to appear in the Book of World Records!

Look, Greedy Smurf, I smurfed the tiniest cake in the world!
!
517

I still smurf that this sport has no future!
zZZz

Look out! Here it comes!
zz
?
© Peyo - 1998 Lic. IMPS (Brussels)

¡OLÉ! ¡OLÉ! ¡OLÉ! ¡OLÉ! ¡OLÉ! ¡OLÉ!
308

Brainy Smurf, I have to smurf you something!
Uh... one moment.

© Peyo - 2003 Lic. IMPS (Brussels)
Well, what? Do you understand what I'm saying?
Yes, yes. That's better.
649

Hey, Dopey Smurf, what are you smurfing? Didn't you see the sign?!
?
?
CAUTION! WET PAINT!
© Peyo - 2001 Lic. IMPS (Brussels)

Well, yeah! I was telling myself it wasn't very smart of you to leave that sign drying on the bench! Someone could've sat on it!
CAUTIO WET PAINT!
445

All right, this is a FORTISSIMO movement!
?
??
?!?
© Peyo - 2002 Lic. IMPS (Brussels)

519
Loud enough to wake up Lazy Smurf!
Oh, okay!
Gotcha!
I see!
That's loud!
WHOA!

And whatever you do, Dopey Smurf, don't cheat!
No, no! 1, 2, 3...

What's he smurfing? We've been waiting for more than an hour!
© Peyo - 1998 Lic. IMPS (Brussels)

1, 2, 3, 4, 6... Uh, no! 1, 2, 3, 4, 5, 8... No, no! 1, 2, 3, 4, 5, 10... Smurf it, no! 1, 2, 3, 4, 7... No! 1, 2, 3...
300

Please... draw me a smurf!
© Peyo

So, how's the experiment going, Papa Smurf?
© Peyo - 1998 Lic. IMPS (Brussels)

191
As you can see, Smurfette, the results are still up in the air!

No, no, no! I want a flower that's pretty and that has a smurfy perfume.
And this one?

Oh, yes! What a scent! Smurfette is going to adore me!
© Peyo - 1998 Lic. IMPS (Brussels)

HELP!
Not just Smurfette! Hee! Hee! Hee!
291

HUP HUP HUP
HUP HUP HUP

© Peyo - 2000 Lic. IMPS (Brussels)

328
?
!

Hey! I forgot I had this smurfy frame!

A lovely frame like this is just asking for a pretty picture... A very pretty picture!

339
I'm going to smurf it into a mirror!

What do you think of the display?
You must have one leg shorter than the other.
272

BRAVO, MAESTRO! ENCORE! ENCORE!!
!
CLAP CLAP
CLAP

Don't you listen to him...
...You know Jokey Smurf. He can't stop himself from spouting smurfiness!
?
485

So, Clumsy Smurf, how's it smurfing?
© Peyo

Me, I don't like the snow!

OOPS!

Oh, that Grouchy Smurf! He's really good at getting all wound up!
358

266

And you're not looking after your garden, Lazy Smurf?
No, Papa Smurf.
© Peyo 1998 - Lic. IMPS (Brussels)

66
All my flowers are plastic.

Here's a cactus for you.
What if I get pricked?
© Peyo - 1998 Lic. IMPS (Brussels)

You'll think of me.
Yes, Dopey Smurf, I will.
151

I just smurfed a new rubbersmurf! It's super bouncy! I smurfed a joke cake out of it.

But where is it? I smurfed it here!
BLOING
BLOING
!

© Peyo - 1998 Lic. IMPS (Brussels)
GREEDY SMURF!
HELP!
BLOING
BLOING
164

Papa Smurf, what happened to you?

I played bluff, and since Papa Smurf cannot tell a lie...
...I lost.
252

What a pack of barbarians! I'll tell Papa Smurf!
BOOOOO!
BOOOoo!

ENCORE! AGAIN! AGAIN!
?
CLAP CLAP CLAP

What do you mean "Encore"? You just smurfed rotten tomatoes at him and you're calling him back?
Yes, I still have three more!
523

I'm really happy I didn't smurf a bet this time.

570
So much suspense is unbearable!
FINISH

BLING
BLING
© Peyo

Are you sure that's how William Tell smurfed it?
Certain, Clumsy Smurf!
© Peyo - 2002 Lic. IMPS (Brussels)
536

And after that, Smurfette, we could smurf a walk in the moonlight!
Yes, okay!

I'm wondering why she accepts your invitations and not mine.
© Peyo - 1998 Lic. IMPS (Brussels)

Come on, it's obvious! I have a much more smurfing physique.
215

I'll leave you behind for sure, Lazy Smurf!
Of course, Dopey Smurf, of course!
© Peyo - 2003 Lic. IMPS (Brussels)
627

Your migraine isn't smurfing any better?

No, I'm in horrible smurf!
Smurf a little of this home remedy and you won't have a headache anymore.
© Peyo - 1998 Lic. IMPS (Brussels)

198

Game, set, and... SMURF!
Women's tennis isn't like it used to be! ≈HFFF...≈ ≈PFFF...≈

Have you heard the latest, Papa Smurf? Lazy Smurf has found something to do!
No way!

It just shows you must never despair.

SMURFS SOUVENIRS
A souvenir shop? But Lazy Smurf, nobody ever smurfs by here!
So what?
121

You shouldn't smurf there, Lazy Smurf! They're calling for a storm!
WHAT? REALLY?

QUICK!

WHEW! Just in time for my big spring cleaning!
637

COSTUME BALL
Being disguised is good, Lazy Smurf. But why as Miller Smurf?

Well, because of the song! You know: "Miller, you're sleepy, your mill smurfs too quickly, Miller, you're sleepy... zZZZ..."
313

What do you smurf of my new style?
Frankly, I'm lost!
91
ART IN THE STREET
STOP

There!
OUCH!
PUNT

Hey, that's enough, isn't it? That's the 15th time since this morning!

...It's like they smurfed the word around!
KICK ME!
113

Papa Smurf, Papa Smurf, I was looking for you...
?

...because I have memory lapses.
Oh, since when?

133
Since when what?

KOF
KOF

© Peyo - 1998 Lic. IMPS (Brussels)
Sorry about your house, Jokey Smurf, but the water's not smurfing any longer!
244

An artist's canvas is infinite.

It's been ten days since April 1st...

© Peyo - 2002 Lic. IMPS (Brussels)
...And Distracted Smurf still hasn't noticed a thing!
566

I've... I've smurfed lots of flowers for Smurfette.
Wonderful, Timid Smurf!

Go smurf them to her right away.
You... You think so?

249
That's so nice, Timid Smurf.

BOP

The boomerang wins again by K.O. against Clumsy Smurf!
383

TWO CHERRIES, PLEASE!

There's no use shouting so loud, I hear you!

There, they were smurfed this morning!
597

256

YIPPEE! I finally smurfed the formula of the smurfoglycerine!

BOOOOM.

Well, now! Papa Smurf is smurfing pranks, too?!
Tsk, tsk, tsk! At his age!
402

So, it's agreed? We'll meet up in a bit to smurf a game?
Agreed!

Where did I smurf that pack of cards? Ah, there it is!

657
Uh... I think we misunderstood one another.
?
!
?

?
© Peyo

Store
BUSINESS HOURS
9:00am
4:00pm

Oh, there you are! Hey, you're not keeping the hours that are smurfed on the sign.
That's right. I change them every day.

I smurf the time when I arrive and when I leave.
OPEN
574

Ready, Flying Smurf?
Yes! Outer space!, here I come!

BOOOM
He must be far away by now!
What are you doing at my home?
417

Look, Brainy Smurf! Baby Smurf is learning the alphabet thanks to those new blocks.

Oh, come on, Smurfette! Surely you know he's still much too young to smurf letters!

I
D
I
O
T
236

Listen up! Our big game is getting started! The girls on one side, the boys on the other!

Do you want my opinion, Sassette? We're starting off with a certain handicap!
372

CRAC
CRAC

CRAC
471

Do me a favor, Greedy Smurf... when you're hungry at night, smurf something besides walnuts!
?

Aha! Signs of wild animals! I'll be able to smurf my tracking talents!

Hmm! Given their depth, it must be a very heavy animal! An elephant? A rhinoceros?
?

I'd say Greedy Smurf, instead!
YUM YUM GULP
CRUNCH
CHOMP CHOMP
BOM BOM BOM BOM
276

Hey, you over there! Those are Brainy Smurf's glasses!
Uh... Yes, Papa Smurf!

How about you go smurf them back to him right now?! He needs them, you know?!
Yes, Papa Smurf!

→Pff!← For once we had some peace!
And like Papa Smurf always says: " Bla... bla... bla... bla..."
398

Ha! Ha! These binoculars are incredible! What a face Hefty Smurf is making, seen from here!

What a schnozz! He's even uglier than a long-nosed monkey! Hee! Hee!

There, I finished smurfing the lenses! We can test out the binoculars...
?
580

POC
POC
POC
NO WALKING ON THE GRASS

TRALA-LA-LA
LALA
?

?
108

Z Z Z

Whoa! It's getting dark already.

It's time for me to go to bed.
310

Okay! Once again I'm trying this formula for a duplication elixir... ⇢Gulp!⇠

DARN!
It's not smurfing! Enough of this!

458
I give up!
© Peyo - 2002 Lic. IMPS (Brussels)

AHHHH!
COSTUME BALL
I don't know what's smurfed into him! I just asked him if he wanted to dance with me!
© Peyo

So, Farmer Smurf? How about that new fertilizer I smurfed for you?
HMMM... MM... MMMM...HM!
© Peyo - 2002 Lic. IMPS (Brussels)
528

Here's the chess game you asked me for, Papa Smurf!

I glued the pieces on because they kept smurfing off!
Thanks, Dopey Smurf.
159

I'm going to smurf a snowman.

ATCHOO!

BROOF

362
!

BZZZ
BZZ
BZZ

BZZ
BZZ
PSHH

PSHH
PSHH
PSHHH

BZZ
BZZZ
BZZ
BZZ
346

Lazy Smurf!
HEY, LAZY SMURF!

It's mean waking me up now! I was smurfing such a nice dream!
Oh, yeah? And what was the dream that was so smurfing?
© Peyo 1998 - Lic. IMPS (Brussels)

I was dreaming I was asleep.
129

-PFFF...- Everything's going fine! What can I smurf in tomorrow's edition?

© Peyo - 2002 Lic. IMPS (Brussels)

506
THE MORNING SMURF
EVERYTHING IS FINE!
BUT FOR HOW MUCH LONGER?

No, there's nothing difficult about it. First, you have to smurf the elastic to the max.

Good job! Now, let it go!
© Peyo - 1998 Lic. IMPS (Brussels)

288
No, Dopey Smurf, your other hand!

334
© Peyo - 2000 Lic. IMPS (Brussels)

No stupid board is going to stop me!
It won't work, Hefty Smurf! It's too warped!

BAM
© Peyo - 2003 Lic. IMPS (Brussels)

There you go! What do you smurf of that?
I'm speech-less.
635

Okay, fine... I think this potion for growing hair doesn't work very well.
© Peyo

?

!

© Peyo - 1998 Lic. IMPS (Brussels)
195

Today, we're going to smurf a new kind of exercise. Pay attention!
© Peyo - 2003 Lic. IMPS (Brussels)

The important thing is to maintain the position for a long time.

591
Good job, Lazy Smurf!
Z

Okay, I'm going to smurf your statue, but you must stay still for a very long time.
© Peyo

Okay... Since I really have to.

But, Papa Smurf, if I smurf the trophy to the winner, what will I console the loser with?
?
434

→Pssst!← Greedy Smurf! Chef Smurf smurfed a cake on his windowsill!
?

Heh! Heh! Heh! Now, quickly to my office!
© Peyo - 1998 Lic. IMPS (Brussels)

Detective Smurf! Someone has stolen my cake!
No problem! I'll see to the matter.
318

You see, Baby Smurf, that caterpillar is a baby like you! And when she grows up, she'll smurf into a butterfly!
© Peyo 1998 - Lic. IMPS (Brussels)

105

Here, Greedy Smurf, what do you think...
Mmm!

...of my soup...
GLUG GLUG

...with cayenne pepper?
96
© Peyo 1998 - Lic. IMPS (Brussels)

I don't feel well. I must be coming down with some-thing...
You play the same smurf on us every time, Lazy Smurf! I'm going to tell Brainy Smurf!

This is a trick for not working on the dam! We're going to call Papa Smurf!
PAPA SMURF!

Well, he really did have a bug this time.
Snirf!
616
© Peyo - 2003 Lic. IMPS (Brussels)

CRUNCH
YUM! YUM! GULP BURP

And you say there's a whole family of worms living in that apple?!
Yes, yes! I promise you! I smurfed it on my windowsill!
GLBLMM...
280
© Peyo - 1998 Lic. IMPS (Brussels)

I'm curious to see if your special fertilizer has smurfed any effect on my peas, Papa Smurf--
LOOK OUT!

?!
BOM
OWW
124
© Peyo 1998 - Lic. IMPS (Brussels)

But I told you not to smurf the WHOLE packet on them, Farmer Smurf!
BOM
BOM
BOM

What are you grrrmurfing, Dopey Grrrmurf?
Papa Grrmurf asked me to grrmurf a fire with these pieces of wood and these rocks...
But it's not grrrmurfing very well!
TAK
TAK
TAK
© Peyo

Ahhhh, Smurfette! Always Smurfette! I can't go a step anymore without smurfing about her!

You see, if this keeps on, she's going to end up driving me CRAZY!
© Peyo - 2000 Lic. IMPS (Brussels)

Jeez, you could answer me when I talk to you, you stupid smurf!
400

Lazy Smurf, that does it! If I see you close your eyes once again today, you're going to smurf it!

?

ZZZ
Unbelievable! He's sleeping with his eyes open!
82

Stamp collecting is smurfily fun!

!

But it's so tiring!
331

?

Hey, you! What's smurfing here?

?
I don't know, Papa Smurf! The last Smurf who knew left ten minutes ago!
462

© Peyo - 1998 Lic. IMPS (Brussels)

© Peyo - 2000 Lic. IMPS (Brussels)

© Peyo - 2001 Lic. IMPS (Brussels)

© Peyo - 2000 Lic. IMPS (Brussels)

© Peyo - 1998 Lic. IMPS (Brussels)

Okay, on your feet!
?

!
I'm not the one you should wake up, it's him.
431

205

...And 9 of spades!
?

Wait... I feel like something really strange is smurfing in this game.
You mean someone is cheating?

643
No... That someone ISN'T cheating!

My clock's ticking keeps me from falling asleep.
I suggest you exchange it for my hourglass.

How's it any better if I have to wake three times a night to turn it over?
220
© Peyo - 1998 Lic. IMPS (Brussels)

I'm smurfily happy with Sculptor Smurf's work!

Mmyeah... I think it's missing a little something...

SPROTCH
!
Ah, there you go! Now it's perfect! Hee! Hee! Hee!
303
© Peyo - 1998 Lic. IMPS (Brussels)

ZZZZZZZZ
My hero!
?
386
© Peyo - 2000 Lic. IMPS (Brussels)

I'm going to smurf a surprise menu for Papa Smurf's birthday!
Mmm! I'd like to know what it'll be.

Can you keep a secret, Greedy Smurf?
Of course!

140
Well then, so can I.

What got me to offer to Papa Smurf to smurf his important message myself?
I'd forgotten you can't rely on storks during the winter.
© Peyo

Let's go have a chat with Fisher Smurf. I think he enjoys my daily visit.

!
HELLO, BRAINY SMURF
YES, IT'S A PERFECT DAY FOR FISHING
NO, THEY'RE NOT BITING
RIGHT, SEE YOU TOMORROW
561

I'm smurfly happy I invented this smurf!

YAAAAAK!
© Peyo - 2000 Lic. IMPS (Brussels)

I'd have been better off by first inventing the weather report!
379

It's too bad, Painter Smurf... Your painting is a complete failure!...
I'm much slimmer than that!
© Peyo

Hmm... I like it a lot!
TAILOR DIPLOMA

It's not too big?
No, no, I'll take it!
TAILOR DIPLOMA
© Peyo - 2002 Lic. IMPS (Brussels)

543

Look... Three arrows, three apples that fell from the tree! Awesome, isn't it?
Yes, it is...
© Peyo - 1998 Lic. IMPS (Brussels)

259
...Especially since that's a pear tree!

BING
BAM
BAM

No thanks, Clumsy Smurf! I don't need any more help!
449
© Peyo - 2001 Lic. IMPS (Brussels)

So much fog! You can't smurf anything more than a step away!
466

BANG
OWW!
OUCH!

Sorry, I didn't smurf you! Do you know where we are?
Yes, near the river!
© Peyo - 2001 Lic. IMPS (Brussels)

Are you sure?
Absolutely! I'm getting out of it!

GRRR!

HIC!
© Peyo 1998 - Lic. IMPS (Brussels)

Nope, that beauty potion still isn't up to snuff.
118

I heard the collision was awful!
He's on the ground, and his face is all smurfed.
?!

427
I couldn't avoid him.

Finally! That famous elixir against memory lapses!
GLUG GLUG

I must smurf the laundry!
Straighten up the lab!
Dig up my garden!
© Peyo - 2000 Lic. IMPS (Brussels)

Hmm... I think I prefer memory lapses.
342

© Peyo

What a splendid block of stone! I feel like I'm going to create a masterpiece out of it.

TOC
TOC
TOC

So, what do you smurf?
Superb, Sculptor Smurf! What purity of form!

I'm going to smash you a good one!

HUMPF!

Oh, wow!
?

?
KLONG

Hey, Smurfs! Look what I smurfed!
Oh! An old pot full of gold coins! Awesome!

It's exactly the kind of pot Smurfette needs for her garden.
As for this gold smurfiness, we'll have to go smurf it into the river again.
57

It seems Papa Smurf is at the lake! I'm going to go smurf him hello.

WHAT?!... Someone has cast a spell on Papa Smurf! Someone has smurfed him into a bush! HELP!

What? I thought I heard Dopey Smurf's voice!
366

Here, Smurfette! I smurfed this little bouquet for you!
?

It's unbelievable! Even Lazy Smurf is affected by the return of Spring!
149

1, 2, 3, 4, 5...
Quick, let's smurf!

Later...
What's strange is we haven't seen Brainy Smurf since that game of hide-'n'-seek!
© Peyo - 2000 Lic. IMPS (Brussels)
I've surely won by now!
394

What have you planned for the annual show, Hefty Smurf?
A demonstration of karate... I'll smurf boards by chopping them with my hand.

Mmyeah, meh... That doesn't sound very smurfing to me.
© Peyo - 1998 Lic. IMPS (Brussels)

295
Uh... All things considered, it sounds perfect.

Clumsy Smurf, I smurfed you not to repair your chair by yourself with my super-glue!
559
© Peyo - 2002 Lic. IMPS (Brussels)

Papa Smurf! I have an idea! What if we smurfed a big party tomorrow?

But we already smurfed one yesterday. We can't smurf a party every two days.
Oh...

Papa Smurf! What if we smurfed one today?
69

Yes, I recently started sculpting in a new style...

I've displayed a piece on the town square, too...

!
349

269

MY GOODNESS!
She's so huge!

602
But, Smurfette, I'm telling you! That ladybug really is huge!
© Peyo - 2003 Lic. IMPS (Brussels)

Z
RELAXATION TRAINING WITH LAZY SMURF
Argh! No! I can't take it anymore! It's too hard!
© Peyo

STOP

© Peyo - 2003 Lic. IMPS (Brussels)

603

Smurfette just fell into the pond!

262
NO!
I don't need anyone to smurf mouth-to-mouth on me!
© Peyo - 1998 Lic. IMPS (Brussels)

Uh... Thanks, Wild Smurf, but...
This isn't exactly what I understood by "What if I smurfed you for a walk in the forest?"
© Peyo

I'm going to go see how Dopey Smurf is managing with the job that I smurfed to him!

OH, NO!

Well, what?! I smurfed like you told me! Half of the eggs on a plate and the other half in the cupboard!
454
© Peyo - 2001 Lic. IMPS (Brussels)

Z
That Lazy Smurf sleeps all the time... It's not normal.

The problem must be psychological. Smurfoanalysis could help him...

© Peyo 1998 - Lic. IMPS (Brussels)
It won't be easy!
ZZZ
77

There it's done! Smurf-time!
Ahh!
Yum!
© Peyo - 1998 Lic. IMPS (Brussels)

YUCK! There's a hair in my soup!

A hair?
182

What a mess! It's high time to sort these papers and to get smurf of what's no longer of any use.
I'll see to it, Papa Smurf...
© Peyo - 2000 Lic. IMPS (Brussels)

354
But first I'll smurf a copy of it... You never know!

?
© Peyo - 2003 Lic. IMPS (Brussels)
606
613
Okay, I'll resmurf my strength and then I'll finally finish this book.

THE SUPER SMURF

Aroo!
He's... he's going to smurf on the ground, it's awful!
Let me, Smurfette!
Oh, no!

Don't move, Baby Smurf, Super Smurf is on the way!

Aroo... Aroo!
Smurf me your hand and you'll be safe...

Oh... he got back down by himself!
HEY! OH!
Hup! Hee-hee!

PLOP
?
You little rascal, I told you not to smurf on the clothesline.
Hee-hee! Aroo!

Honestly, Super Smurf, I think you should change smurfs, because you have no talent for this.

No talent... no talent... I'll prove to them I really am a Super Smurf!

CHEEEEP! CHEEEEP! CHEEEEP!
!

CHEEP
CHEEP
CHEEP
That chick has left its nest. It doesn't know how to smurf yet... It... it's going to fall!
© Peyo
2

You're lucky, little smurf. Super Smurf is here to save you! Come this way.
CHEEP
CHEEEEP
CHEEP

KRAK
CHEEP
CHEEEEP

PLOP

I wonder if Jokey Smurf was right... I'm not talented...

EEEEEEEEK! HELP!
?

HA! HA! HA! Good catch! A little blond creature with a dress and a white cap! This must be that Smurfette Gargamel told me about!
?
I'm not a Smurfette!

I'm the fairy Cloclo! You're mistaken. I'm not a Smurfette, I tell you!

Little liar, I'm sure Gargamel will give me a nice reward for capturing you!
Let me go! EEEE!

EEEK! Help!
Keep shouting! Heh-heh!
She dropped her magic wand.

If I dared... Maybe I could save the fairy!

ABRACADABRA! I WANT TO BE A SUPER SMURF!
BOP

POOF

HURRAY! It worked! I'm a Super Smurf!
© Peyo
3

And to reward you for saving me, by the power of this magic kiss, I swear to you that, from now on, in my heart, you'll be a Super Smurf!

Really? Thanks, but I... Uh--

SMAK

4

END

W.\^TCH OUT FO.:

Welcome to the fun-filled, frivolous, fourth volume of THE SMURFS TALES by Peyo—brought to you by Papercutz, those very serious characters dedicated to publishing great graphic novels for all ages. I'm Jim Salicrup, Papercutz Smurf-in-Chief and Archivist for the Peewit Papers (Peewit's important personal diaries and such), here to once again pontificate and reflect on all things Smurf...

Like in most of the *Watch Out for Papercutz* columns found in THE SMURFS TALES, I try to reveal bits of fascinating behind-the-scenes info regarding the Smurfs. If you've been faithfully picking up every volume of THE SMURFS TALES then you already know the story of the Man Who Created the Smurfs—young Belgian cartoonist Pierre Culliford, better known to the world by his penname Peyo! You know that when he was creating a Johan and Peewit adventure—a comics series that he wrote and drew—that in one particular story, published way back in 1958, he introduced a village profusely populated with dozens of blue elves, who came to be known in America as the Smurfs. That story, of course, has been re-presented in the second graphic novel of THE SMURFS published by Papercutz. And that story was re-re-presented in the larger-sized SMURFS ANTHOLOGY Volume One, which featured bonus behind-the-scenes info from our very own Smurfologist, Matt. Murray. And that story has also been re-re-re-presented most recently in Volume One of THE SMURFS 3 IN 1 (which also included the stories from THE SMURFS #1 and #3).

That story, which originally ran in legendary Belgian comics magazine *Spirou*—issue number 1047, May 8, 1958, to be precise—was "*La Flûte à six trous*" ("The Flute with Six Holes") was also adapted into the very first Smurfs film, *The Smurfs and the Magic Flute* in 1976. But while that story indeed introduced us to *les Schtroumpfs*, as the Smurfs were originally called (and still are in several countries), some Smurfs fan have wondered exactly when Johan met Peewit? Well, have we got good news! Collected within this volume of THE SMURFS TALES is the story that answers that question. Originally entitled *"Le lutin du Bois aux Roches,"* "The Goblin of Rocky Wood" is the tale that brings our heroes together for the first time. And, unlike the repeatedly reprinted "The Smurfs and the Magic Flute," this is the first time we're presenting this classic tale in a Papercutz graphic novel.

But then again, most of what we present in THE SMURFS TALES is being published here by Papercutz for the first time, with a few notable exceptions. For example, in our previous, much-acclaimed volume, we re-presented the two previous out-of-print Papercutz graphic novels that featured the female Smurfs of Smurfy Grove along with the newest graphic novel to feature those fabulous femmes. And even in this volume, we're re-presenting "The Super Smurf," which technically was never before in a Papercutz graphic novel—it appeared in a Smurfs FREE COMIC BOOK DAY comic from Papercutz.

THE SMURFS TALES is mainly dedicated to continuing to bringing you all the Smurfs graphic novels that we haven't yet published, as well as other Peyo-created characters such as *Johan and Peewit* and *Benny Breakiron*. And if that wasn't enough, we've also been able to bring you the Smurfs comic strips known as *The Smurf Gags*. We think this makes THE SMURFS TALES the perfect publication for all Peyo fans. That doesn't mean we're neglecting the millions of new Smurf-fans that have only recently discovered our little blue buddies on their new Nickolodeon animated TV series. For them, there's THE SMURFS 3 IN 1 series, which is collecting three volumes of the original Papercutz SMURFS graphic novels into each volume of the aptly named THE SMURFS 3 IN 1.

So, between the new TV series (not to mention the original animated series which is still available—even on its own YouTube channel) and all the Papercutz SMURFS graphic novels, you'd think you'd have enough to satisfy any appetite for Smurfs, even Gargamel's! But you'd be wrong, which is why new Smurfs TV episodes are being developed even as we speak, and we're hard at work putting together the next volumes of THE SMURFS 3 IN 1 and THE SMURFS TALES. We're doing all we can to make sure that you'll be able to stay Smurfy!

Smurf you later,

Jim

STAY IN TOUCH!

EMAIL:	salicrup@papercutz.com
WEB:	papercutz.com
TWITTER:	@papercutzgn
INSTAGRAM:	@papercutzgn
FACEBOOK:	PAPERCUTZGRAPHICNOVELS
FANMAIL:	Papercutz, 160 Broadway, Suite 700 East Wing, New York, NY 10038

Go to papercutz.com and sign up for the free Papercutz e-newsletter!

MORE GRAPHIC NOVELS AVAILABLE FROM charmz™

STITCHED #1
"THE FIRST DAY OF THE REST OF HER LIFE"

STITCHED #2
"LOVE IN THE TIME OF ASSUMPTION"

G.F.F.s #1
"MY HEART LIES IN THE 90s"

G.F.F.s #2
"WITHCES GET THINGS DONE"

CHLOE #1
"THE NEW GIRL"

CHLOE #2 "THE QUEEN OF HIGH SCHOOL"

CHLOE #3
"FRENEMIES"

CHLOE #4
"RAINY DAY"

SCARLET ROSE #1
"I KNEW I'D MEET YOU"

SCARLET ROSE #2
"I'LL GO WHERE YOU GO"

SCARLET ROSE #3
"I THINK I LOVE YOU"

SCARLET ROSE #4
"YOU WILL ALWAYS BE MINE"

AMY'S DIARY #1
"SPACE ALIEN... ALMOST?"

SWEETIES #1
"CHERRY SKYE"

MONICA ADVENTURES #1

ANA AND THE COSMIC RACE #1
"THE RACE BEGINS"

Charmz graphic novels are available for $9.99 in paperback, and $14.99 in hardcover. Available from booksellers everywhere. You can also order online from www.papercutz.com. Or call 1-800-886-1223, Monday through Friday, 9–5 EST. MC, Visa, and AmEx accepted. To order by mail, please add $5.00 for postage and handling for first book ordered, $1.00 for each additional book and make check payable to NBM Publishing. Send to: Charmz, 160 Broadway, Suite 700, East Wing, New York, NY 10038. Charmz graphic novels are also available wherever e-books are sold.